G R JORDAN

Cobra's Fang

A Contessa Munroe Mystery

First published by Carpetless Publishing 2021

Copyright © 2021 by G R Jordan

All rights reserved. No part of this publication may be reproduced, stored or transmitted in any form or by any means, electronic, mechanical, photocopying, recording, scanning, or otherwise without written permission from the publisher. It is illegal to copy this book, post it to a website, or distribute it by any other means without permission.

This novel is entirely a work of fiction. The names, characters and incidents portrayed in it are the work of the author's imagination. Any resemblance to actual persons, living or dead, events or localities is entirely coincidental.

G R Jordan asserts the moral right to be identified as the author of this work.

G R Jordan has no responsibility for the persistence or accuracy of URLs for external or third-party Internet Websites referred to in this publication and does not guarantee that any content on such Websites is, or will remain, accurate or appropriate.

Designations used by companies to distinguish their products are often claimed as trademarks. All brand names and product names used in this book and on its cover are trade names, service marks, trademarks and registered trademarks of their respective owners. The publishers and the book are not associated with any product or vendor mentioned in this book. None of the companies referenced within the book have endorsed the book.

First edition

ISBN: 978-1-914073-35-9

This book was professionally typeset on Reedsy.
Find out more at reedsy.com

The cobra will bite you whether you
call it cobra or Mr. Cobra

INDIAN PROVERB

Contents

Foreword

This story is set in numerous towns and cities throughout Europe. Any persons named are entirely fictional, as are the events and specific places. If the UK had not decided to depart from the European Union, I firmly believe Catriona may have caused Europe to depart from us!

Acknowledgement

To Susan, Jean and Rosemary for your work in bringing this novel to completion, your time and effort is deeply appreciated.

1

Chapter 01

'Now, wait till you see what's in this box, Tiff.'

Catriona slid out a box that was ornate on the outside with an eagle carved into it. She fumbled around the edges, locating the secret switch that would pop the box open, but something was unusual. Something was off. Normally, she would simply push it gently on the right-hand side of the box, the switch being just below where the box separated, but it was already indented. On closure, the switch should pop back out and form an almost seamless seal with the edge of the box. You would have to trace very carefully with your hands to know it was there, but now it was pushed in. It had stayed in even though the box itself was shut.

'Why are you showing me this?' asked Tiff.

'I told you, this is my jewellery collection. A lot of these are what Luigi gave me.' Luigi was Catriona's deceased husband, an Italian Count whom she had married despite the protestations of both families. Unfortunately, the man collapsed and died whilst on holiday, and now, Catriona lived a life where she spent Luigi's family's money but maintained the promise of never coming to visit them. It was far from ideal. Certainly not the happy family life that she had always wanted. Not that her own family was much better. Tiff, her niece, had been dropped on Catriona as a companion, someone who was not wanted by the family either. Although their comments that Tiff was on the spectrum were accurate, Catriona found her to be a most amicable companion after their initial false starts.

'Tiff, there's something wrong with this box; look.' Catriona watched her niece look over her shoulder.

'You meant to press that in?' asked Tiff.

'Yes. That's the secret button. You press that and you're able to open up the box, but it shouldn't be stuck in like that.'

'Certainly not very secret when you put it that way,' said Tiff. 'I think it's broken.'

'Thanks for that,' said Catriona, 'but it shouldn't be. It wasn't broken the last time I touched it.'

'How long ago was that?'

'Over a month. Except . . . no, it was over a month. I am right. I haven't been near this box since.'

'There can't be much in it you want to show people then,' said Tiff.

'We haven't been here. When was the last time we were back here with the family on the estate? I feel I don't know Scotland anymore, we get to be here so little.'

This was an exaggeration. Catriona had lived away from the family for a short period with her husband. Since he died, she had returned only briefly and this visit was intended to be a short stop, too. It was good to see the family on occasion but spend too long and being good to see them turned to rows and fights and comments about her fitness to act as a Contessa.

Maybe that was the crux of it, thought Catriona. Maybe it was the jealousy that she had a real title. Her father would trace the family back to the great Munros, but the great Munros spelt their name differently. Catriona's family were not part of the heritage who had once walked around the Scottish hills and lakes. Instead, her family had come from America. She was probably more closely related to the famous movie star than they were to any clan chief.

'It opens,' said Catriona. 'Look, Tiff, it's open.' Gently, she pushed the lid back. Inside, a number of jewels shone back.

'There's an awful lot in there,' said Tiff. 'How do you wear all those at once?'

'You don't wear them at once. You pick and choose, but there's one in here that's my favourite—one that Luigi gave to me. It was very personal between the two of us.'

'Where is it?' asked Tiff.

'It'll be in here. Let me just pull this compartment back, and it will be—Oh, it's not there!'

'What did it look like?'

'It's a snake. A snake with an emerald. It hangs on a chain from my neck. Luigi called it the cobra's fang. Apparently, it was much sought after. But it should be in here somewhere.' With that, Catriona began to lift each of the jewels, necklaces, earrings, and brooches and placed them on the table. Within a minute, some twenty items lay there. The cobra's fang was not among them.

'Tiff, it's not there. Where the hell is it, Tiff? Where is it? This box lid was open.'

'You didn't just misplace it? I mean, you're not the cleverest at times, are you?'

'Shut up, Tiff, now is not the time to be smart. It's not there.'

'Then don't touch the box,' said Tiff. 'If you touch the box, you'll contaminate the fingerprints. If somebody's taken it, they might have left prints. They might have left a hair.'

'Taken? Stolen? Surely not,' said Catriona. 'Surely it will be left somewhere, but I didn't have it out. I haven't worn it since . . . Well, I did wear it at the funeral, but it wasn't on show. It was underneath my top. I wore it because I thought Luigi would want me to, but it's a bit strange. I came back, picked you up, left it here, and it was locked away. Locked away in the box, I mean. We haven't really kept these jewels anywhere else, have we? The family doesn't own enough to be a serious target for robbery. We don't have that much.'

'How much was it worth?' asked Tiff.

'Don't be so crass; it's worth everything. Luigi gave it to me.'

'It might be worth a lot to you, but what was it worth? You see, if somebody's going to take it, it has to be worth something, doesn't it?'

'It was nothing,' said Catriona. 'Luigi bought it for me on a whim. The fact was he didn't even want me to show it to his family, said it was probably beneath them. Less than what they expected. But he thought it would look good on me. He liked to watch me wearing it when we were together. Properly together, Tiff, not like a dinner or anything.'

'And that's too much detail,' said Tiff. 'I don't need to know what you wore with him when you were up to whatever, but what was it worth?'

'I told you, I don't know, but it can't be worth much if he didn't want me to put it on display. You know how Luigi's family always ranked money, ostentatious displays of this and that. It's one of the reasons he said he liked me, my dislike of showing off.'

'I hope there are more reasons than that. It's pretty lame, really, isn't it?' said Tiff.

Catriona smiled. You could always rely on Tiff for an uplifting comment, but then Cat's face furrowed again. *Where was it?*

Catriona systematically emptied the desk she was sitting at. She would never have put anything in any of the other drawers, but she wanted to be sure, and then she went to the family safe to make sure it was not in there either. That was where the more expensive jewels were kept—not that she had a lot of them, but her mother had a few, or at least ones she thought were expensive.

All the items that were meant to be in the safe were there with no extras. Catriona's father was in the lounge sitting in front of a large fire. As Tiff and Catriona entered the room, he rustled the paper indicating he did not wish to be disturbed but Cat took the bull by the horns, marched over, and pulled the paper down so she could see her father's face.

'Did you lock up any of my jewellery?' she asked.

'No. It's your jewellery, and you look after it. You haven't gone and lost it, have you?' His tone was gruff, but then it had always been. He was a man used to business decisions and telling things as they were, which is why his deluded ideas about being part of the clan Munro got to Catriona. It was so unlike him. Maybe it had come from Mother, but either way, they seemed to want to be aristocracy and yet they could not handle it when she married an Italian, even if he was an Italian with a title.

'There's an item that Luigi gave me, very dear to me, Father, but I can't find it. I was wondering if you'd put it away anywhere.'

'I don't go in your room when you're not here. I don't go in your room when you are here. If you don't put it in the safe, this is what happens. You misplace it and you lose it.'

'And if you put it in a safe, you never wear it,' said Catriona, shaking her head and leaving the room. She heard the rustle of the paper going back up and knew in the next minute her father would be satisfied again, having shuffled himself back into the chair.

'I'm going to call the police,' said Cat. 'I'm going to call the police, Tiff, and see if anything has been going on.'

'Do you think that's wise?' asked Tiff.

'What do you mean, "Is that wise?" Something's been stolen, involve the police.'

'Well, you don't know it's been stolen. Do you?' queried Tiff. 'You could have lost it. You get absentminded and lose it. You are getting older.'

'Tiff, I'm twenty-five, in the middle twenties. I am not an old age pensioner. Just because I happen to be slightly older than you.'

'Oh, the mind can go at any time and you have been under a lot of stress ever since Luigi passed on. My money's on you putting it somewhere absentmindedly.'

With that vote of confidence, Catriona girded herself for the phone call to the police. The man who answered the call was courteous and advised that an officer would be dispatched shortly. It was an hour later when Catriona welcomed a sergeant and a constable into the large drawing room and offered them a seat in front of another roaring fire.

'Now then, Contessa, if I could just take some details. You are Contessa Munroe. Where does that name come from?'

'It's from my father. My name is Contessa Catriona Cullodena Munroe and my husband was a Count, Luigi. The Count de Los Palermo.'

Catriona could tell something was wrong by the way the eyes shifted between the sergeant and the constable.

'He was your husband, you say?' The sergeant shuffled his hands, looking around him. 'The item you're looking for, ma'am? What is it?'

'It's a necklace. A snake, and it has a green emerald on it. Luigi called it the cobra's fang. He liked me to wear it, but the last time I wore it was at his funeral, after which I came back here and it was put away in the box. The box was in the drawer but I found it stuck open with the secret button pushed in. Somebody's been tampering with it.'

'Somebody indeed, ma'am, and your husband tampered with it first.'

'I'm sorry,' said Catriona. 'I don't understand.'

'I think he means it was nicked already,' said Tiff. Catriona flashed a glare at her niece.

'I got that, Tiff; thank you very much. What do you mean, Sergeant, that the item was already stolen?'

'I'm afraid so, ma'am. That particular piece was stolen from an Italian bank some ten years ago. It would appear that your husband was either a fence for it or a thief. His name has come up in the past regarding this particular item. I did a little research before we came out, realised who your husband was. If I'm honest, he's a rather unsavoury character in this, linked to a large number of stolen items. Possibly the chickens have come home to roost.'

'How dare you!' said Catriona. 'Luigi was an upstanding man, full of fun, full of life, but there was nothing devious about him. He kept no secrets from me.'

'Or so you thought,' said Tiff.

'Enough, Tiff. Luigi kept no secrets from me. This must be a mistake. I'd like you to investigate, Sergeant.'

'Oh, we'll investigate, all right, ma'am. I'm just saying that this stolen item seems to have been in your possession. You could be an accessory.'

'I doubt Luigi would have stolen it. He must have bought it from someone. It must have got into the system. I'd kindly request that you didn't sully my husband's name.'

The sergeant got to his feet, followed by the constable, walked over to Catriona, and lifted his hat.

'We'll get on with our inquiries, ma'am, but I have to tell you, your view of your husband and that from the file in the police station are so widely different, I'm beginning to wonder if it's the same man.' With that the man turned on his heel, leaving the room.

'Can you believe that, Tiff? Can you believe it? Saying that Luigi would have kept me in the dark.'

'It's not an uncommon practice amongst husbands.'

'Shut up. What do you know about married life?'

'Well, I've read plenty,' said Tiff.

'Again, what do you know about married life?' yelled Catriona and leant forward, putting her hands over her face. They stayed there as the first tears came from her eyes.

2

Chapter 02

Catriona stood on the veranda of the family home, looking out across the heather-covered fields that led into the mountains in the distance. Had she really not known her husband? Was Luigi so much more than he ever said he was? She couldn't believe he was a thief. He kept nothing from her. Those short days of their life together had certainly been intense, but they had also been open. He had spoken of everything. He talked about his hopes and dreams, where he had come from, and she still remembered him giving her the cobra's fang. It was given with sincerity, given to his lover, to the one he was hoping to be with, to stay with. This must all be a mistake. Surely, this was a mistake.

The family had arrived for dinner, her father grumpy after a difficult day at his work. Her father ran several businesses. One thing about him was when business was going well, he was a cheery sort of man, but when it wasn't, as seemed to be happening much more often, he got grumpy.

Her mother was never impressed with Cat. When she saw

9

her brother arrive, Tiffany's father, Cat knew that her mother would be fawning over him. The constant remarks at dinner had left Catriona in no doubt what she had felt as a child, felt as a teenager, and a grown woman. They thought she was just some slap-dash lucky sponger living off the proceeds of a dead husband. And Mother wondered why Cat never came home to visit her.

Tiffany had been at dinner as well, but in some ways, it was like she was ignoring her father. Tiff had barely eaten and then had excused herself from the table to disappear to her room. In fact, she hadn't excused herself at all. She had merely got up, and when Catriona's father had asked what the problem was, there had been a quick mention of something unintelligible before Tiff left the room.

Catriona's mother exclaimed in disgust that Cat was being a poor influence on Tiff. She surely was not this ignorant when the pair had left. With regards to social graces, Tiff was as ignorant as she had always been. Catriona had long decided she was not going to be able to deal with that side of Tiff's life. Instead, she was trying to get to know her niece, build her up, since no one else in the family seemed willing to deal with the girl and help her with her autism. Certainly, from the family point of view, both were little runts that the family could not shake off.

There was a knock at the bedroom door. Cat came back in from the veranda that adjoined her bedroom and opened the large wooden door of her room. She could see a policeman standing with a cap in hand.

'My apologies, ma'am; they said this is where you would be. I didn't realise it was your bedroom. If we could speak outside, maybe?'

'Not all officer, come with me,' said Catriona, extending a finger and indicating that the man should follow, taking him across the room out to the veranda.

'That's quite the view,' said the officer, 'but I'm afraid I have some bad news for you.'

'Really?' said Catriona. 'The investigation's not going well, then?'

'We tracked down a gentleman, who was seen in the vicinity of this estate, but unfortunately, we cannot tie him to any illegal action. However, the fact that he was here is suspicious in its own right.'

'Who is this man?'

'I'm afraid we're being very careful about handing out the name. You are, after all, a potential suspect.'

'I doubt I'm a suspect in stealing my own property.'

'It wasn't your property to begin with, was it?' asked the officer.

'Let's not get caught up on semantics. It was given to me in good faith and I'm sure my husband bought it as such. Now, who is this man?' demanded Catriona, raising herself up to as great a height as she could. She still failed to dominate the officer, a trim gentleman, but at least six feet tall.

'Really, ma'am, I can't.'

Catriona turned and shuffled her way across the veranda. 'It's affected me greatly. I hope you understand that. Some sort of closure, some sort of way of knowing what had happened would be greatly appreciated. Anything you can tell me.' Catriona sniffed. She allowed her hands to shake, her shoulders slumped. She turned, tears falling from her eyes, and then looked up slowly to the man, her hair falling down around her face.

'I guess it wouldn't do any harm. It's a German fellow, Matthias. Matthias Weiner, a professional thief that we know resides on the Isle of Mull, although currently he's not there. We did send officers to investigate and interview the man, but he seems to have disappeared sometime in the last week. He was seen here, around this building, three to four weeks ago. The item that's gone missing would be a prime candidate for someone like him, but you'd also need to know he was here. As we understand it from your earlier comments, the jewel was given to you by your husband and you kept it in your jewellery box. As you haven't worn it that often, recently, I find it quite surprising that the man would know you have it unless your husband was involved with him.'

Cat sniffed, but the look she gave the man left him in no doubt at her anger at the comment.

'I'm sorry, ma'am,' said the officer. 'It is our belief that the Count may have been involved in a group of rather high-class robbers who were committing burglaries of a highly organised kind. Specific items, jewels of high value. It was this group that took the cobra's fang from a bank in Italy some ten years ago. We're unsure as to quite what involvement your husband had, but he certainly must have been able to get his hands on the goods. Those we have interviewed said he was a likable man. A group of robbers, like Matthias, need someone with a name behind them to get access to places. We do know your husband had an account in the bank.'

'My husband had accounts in banks all over the world. He was the Count de Los Palermo, with substantial family wealth. Of course, he had bank accounts. What does that prove?'

'Nothing in and of itself, ma'am, but be aware, we do know he knew Matthias Weiner. There were several photographs from some years ago of the two at various locations, parties, social events. As I said, this group ran amongst the high class of clientele, those who had jewels of significant worth. But so far, it's run cold. If anything else comes up on the trail, we will let you know, but as far as we are aware in this country, the cobra's fang is gone as is Mr. Weiner and that's where it's gone cold. But, we will be looking into your husband's past in a much deeper fashion.'

'And you'll find nothing,' said Cat, letting tears fall from her eyes. 'Luigi was a good man.'

There came a knock at the door. Catriona went to walk across to it but the door opened, and she saw Tiff walk in—jumper and jeans—and promptly throw herself on Cat's bed.

'Now is not a good time, Tiff,' said Cat.

'Why?'

'The officer was still speaking to me.'

'What about?'

'Tiff. It's not a time for a conversation.'

'Why?'

Catriona realised that this was not going to go anywhere until Tiff had some sort of an answer. Surely, she could see the tears in Catriona's face, albeit half put on to encourage sympathy from the officer.

'The officer was saying that they've been unable to recover my jewel. The cobra's fang, he believes, is out of the country along with the German gentleman they reckon may have stolen it. A Matthias Weiner. He's just advising me that they will still continue to look into dearest Luigi, but they're going to do little else in regards to finding my personal property.'

'I'm sorry you're taking it that way,' said the officer. 'If you don't mind, I'll excuse myself. I may have more questions for you so don't be surprised if we call.'

The man turned on his heel and departed, allowing Cat to wipe the tears from her eyes. Tiff was no longer looking at her, instead lying back on the bed, and had picked up a magazine from the side. She looked through it and Catriona began to shake her head. She rushed over to the bed, put her hand on the magazine, pulled it from Tiff and threw it on the floor.

'What are we going to do?'

'What do you mean?' asked Tiff. 'We've had dinner, haven't we? Is there anything else to do?'

'Not about dinner, not about the family,' said Catriona, 'but what that officer just said.'

'What did he say?'

'Tiff, weren't you listening? They're not going to find it. They're not going to find the cobra's fang. It's gone. Luigi gave me that. Somebody has taken one of the last few things I have of my husband. You don't realise what that jewel means to me.'

'No. You're right,' said Tiff. 'I don't. It's just jewellery.'

'No, it isn't,' said Cat. She grabbed Tiff by the arm, dragging her across and right onto the veranda. 'Look. Look around you.'

Tiffany stretched and stared out, checking the mountains in the distance, listening to the river running through the estate.

'Where is this?' said Catriona.

'It's Scotland, isn't it? You know that.'

'It's Scotland. Exactly,' said Catriona. 'Luigi's not here. He didn't come from here. We didn't spend any time here. Even over in Italy, we spent little time at his estates and grounds. In our short time together, we moved around. That necklace, these little bits and pieces I have. It's all I have of him. There's nothing else, Tiff. I need to get that back. It's like I still have a part of Luigi if I have it.'

'But Luigi's dead,' said Tiff. 'I mean it's just a necklace. It doesn't—'

Catriona grabbed her by the shoulders, pulled her close. 'Yes, it does. You may not have a clue about this. You may not understand. God knows you can't be empathetic with anyone. But it matters. Get it into your thick head. It matters. You don't have to understand it. You don't have to tell me you agree with it. You just have to understand, Tiff. It matters.'

Catriona stared into the blank expression on Tiff's face. The eyes were trying to look somewhere else. She was shaking her shoulders, trying to free the grip of Catriona.

'Okay. I get it. So, you need this. You need this jewel for whatever reason. So, what are you gonna do about it?' asked Tiff.

'What are we going to do about it? You're the one with the brain. You're the one who understands all this mystery stuff. Not me. We're going to get the jewel. You tell me how we get it.'

Most people would have looked blankly, shrugged their shoulders, told Catriona that this task was not for them, but instead, Tiff turned away and strode rather thoughtfully looking out at the countryside beyond.

'We won't find it here. I know that,' said Tiff.

'Well, thanks,' said Catriona. 'I kind of got that bit. The police said Matthias Weiner was on the Isle of Mull. That's all we've got really, isn't it?'

'You don't know anybody that Luigi ran with in this criminal gang?'

'He is not a criminal. He did not run with them. I don't know how they even tied him to them.'

'Well, we've got Matthias Weiner,' said Tiff. 'That's a link. And we've also got the bank the cobra's fang was stolen from, which Luigi had an account in. That is our link.'

'So, what do we do about it?' said Cat.

'We go, we investigate, and we find out. We pull up everything we can about it then work out what's important and what isn't. I can do that. Don't worry about that. I'll do that for you.'

'So, we need to go to the Isle of Mull,' said Cat. 'We need to go and hunt down this Matthias Weiner that the police cannot find.'

'Exactly,' said Tiff. 'And how hard have they even looked? They don't care about this, do they? They think your husband was a crook.'

'He was not a crook.'

'Well, he certainly hasn't proved to be a crook,' said Tiff.

'Tiff, your uncle was not a crook. Would you show a bit of family loyalty for once?'

'I'm just being dispassionate, trying to look at things from all sides.'

'Well, turn your face and look in the direction of the Isle of Mull because that's where we're going.'

'Father said we were stopping here for another couple of days. He was possibly going to take me back to his own place for a while.'

'You want to go home?' asked Cat. 'You want to go home and sit there and be berated for being strange and weird?'

'Of course not,' said Tiff, 'but that's what we're doing.'

'No, we're not,' said Cat. 'We're going to Isle of Mull. Go to your room, pack a bag. I'll pack mine and see you downstairs, in an hour and a half's time. It's time for a little road trip. Nobody but nobody calls my husband a crook. There's a reasonable explanation behind this, and I'm going to find it.'

3

Chapter 03

Tiff placed their baggage in the back of the car before joining Cat, who was waiting impatiently behind the wheel. After Tiff slammed the door, Cat put the foot down on the accelerator, and together they drove the small Nissan Micra out of the family estate. The sun was beginning to descend, and shadows stretched across the hills around them.

'Couldn't we have just gone in the morning?' asked Tiff. 'It would be a lot better; we can't even get a ferry across tonight, by the time we drive down.'

'I think it will take us a good four, maybe five hours, to get there, but you go ahead and sleep if you're tired, Tiff. I've got to make a stop off first anyway.'

'Why? Do we need any food with us? Are you getting any sweets?'

'It's not food I'm thinking of. We're heading off to the thief's house; we need to know where Mathias Weiner lives, Tiff. Without that, we'll just be driving around the Mull looking for some random stranger.'

'I kind of hoped you might have that detail. You never mentioned the issue before.'

'It's because I will have that detail. I used to date an ex-policeman around here and I gave him a call. He's always glad to see me. That's the thing, Tiff, you need to be able to do the social side as well. See, you're not a bad-looking lass—you could probably work this side of things, too.'

Tiff give dagger eyes at Catriona. No, there's no way she'd sully herself for any man, thought Cat. She's probably ashamed of the notion that I would, but I need this . . . no, we need this address to clear Luigi's name.

The car trundled along until darkness fell. Catriona pulled in at a layby, somewhere along the A9 and in the shadows she could see a car in the distance. Once she had parked up, she flashed the headlights at the car occupant, and sat, waiting for someone to approach. A man stepped out of the car, but she could barely make his features in the dark, but as he got closer, she remembered the imposing size of the man.

Angus had been the one all the girls had liked at school; his name was the one they mentioned when they excitedly chatted about who could take them to the prom. Of course, it wasn't called the prom in those days—it was simply the end-of-year dance; prom was too American a word. Catriona had been the standout, probably because she was the new girl. She had briefly arrived back from America, spending six months in Scotland before being whizzed away again. Maybe that's what did it for Angus. Cat preferred to think of the fact that she had the looks, the long flowing dark hair, a shapely figure, and maybe, just maybe she was just different—a standout.

She had an American twang back then, one that her father

adored but which she quickly got rid of, once she'd arrived back. Angus had asked her to the dance and she turned him down, because ultimately, he was pretentious, arrogant, thought himself God's gift to women. Yet he never stopped trying for the rest of the six months. She'd even received a message from him around her wedding day, though she did not know how he'd found out a number to contact her on. Well, he was police, or maybe he just knew how to use his contacts in an irregular fashion. Catriona certainly hoped so.

As he made his way to the car, she carefully ran her fingers through her hair, licked her lips and did her best to take the sleep out of her eye that had come from driving too long.

The door opened and there stood an older face than she remembered. Angus had been young and handsome, strong limbed. Now he was still large, but had a potbelly. She thought he would have been in better shape, but then again, maybe she wasn't.

He was standing, holding the door open, so Cat stepped out, hoping that the tight jeans and jumper she was wearing would be enough, banking on his previous affection, hoping that she wouldn't have to entice him any more than her smart but casual outfit was offering. Part of her didn't know how far she would go to obtain this address, and she sure as heck didn't want to find out.

As Cat stepped out of the car, she leaned back against the rear door, and allowed Angus to put his hand just above her shoulder.

'You haven't changed a bit, have you?' said the man, taking in her full figure.

You have, and it's not for the better, she thought but Cat raised her hand up the side of her head and pushed her hair back.

'Been too long,' she said.

'I'm sorry it didn't work out with that Italian man. Tragic,' said Angus, but the insincerity in his voice was clear. 'What have you been doing with yourself?'

'I'm just back, trying to find out where I am, what's going on, see how I feel.'

'If you're in the neighbourhood, maybe some time we can get a drink.'

'Maybe,' said Cat. 'Maybe a bit more for old time's sake. What's your number? I mean, your mobile number, not the one I've got for you at the station.'

Angus reeled off his number, writing it down on a scrap of paper before taking it and placing it in Catriona's hands. He clutched his own, over hers and sniffed. 'You smell good,' he said. 'But you always did.'

'Did you find out what I needed to know?'

'Here,' he said, placing a second piece of paper into Catriona's hands. 'Don't be a stranger too long,' he said. 'Ring me.' He pushed himself forward, placing his lips against hers, kissing her hard. Catriona nearly reared but she accepted his kiss, returning it with fake gusto, before sliding herself back inside the car. Once he shut the door, she flipped on the lights, pressed the accelerator, and drove off into the darkness of the A9, looking to cut across country to Oban.

'You like him then?' asked Tiff.

Cat rolled down the window and spat. 'There's things you have to do in life. Creep.' All right. She wouldn't be seeing him again. 'Tiff, there's no way I'll be seen dead with that man, but we have an address and we have the night to drive with a ferry to catch in the morning. So, so far, it's been a successful night's work.'

'I wouldn't kiss a man just for something like that.'

'Tiff, you've never had a husband. You've barely had a boyfriend. Don't tell me what you would and wouldn't do for someone.'

'There would be other ways to do it that I would think of.' Catriona let her talk off into the night. She wasn't listening anymore. Her niece's drones mere background noise as she stared along the road, lit up by her car headlights. The Isle of Mull was a long drive away but Cat didn't feel tired. She felt angry. Someone had besmirched Luigi's name; someone was calling him a thief. Someone would pay.

The two women slummed it that night in a carpark on the south side of Oban, before making their way to the ferry. Tiff had popped out to grab a couple of bacon rolls, but Catriona was still hungry as they docked on the Isle of Mull, disembarking at Craignure, and taking a quick glance at the sound of Mull they had come along. Catriona was feeling positive.

'So where are we going?' asked Tiff. 'Where exactly is this house?'

'It's on the south side of the island, just beyond Bunessan. Have you ever been on Mull?'

'No,' said Tiff, 'but I can look it up on Google.' Within seconds, Tiff had the map of the island on her mobile screen.

Cat rolled down her window and breathed in the air. 'It's nice here,' she said. 'Pleasant. Plenty of countryside, trees. You feel like you're lost and away from it. Similar in some ways to Italy or maybe that's just everywhere.'

'What are you on about? There's nothing here,' said Tiff. 'There's no big cities or nothing. They just have those funny-coloured houses. Every time you look up Mull, you get these funny multi-coloured houses along a bay.'

'That's up the other end, Tobermory. We're going to the south end, so just sit back. It won't be more than an hour.'

After they had passed through the small village of Bunessan, the road drifted along by the shore before Cat had to make a sharp turn. As she kept driving, she pointed out through the window, shouting at Tiff to take a look. 'That's it up there, off the road in the middle of the field,' she said. 'Hard to get to without being seen.'

'We need to park away from it,' said Tiff. 'I'll take over from now. You find somewhere for us to park—I'll get us inside.'

'You're going to get us inside?'

'Of course. Not a problem. Park somewhere up here. I've got some stuff in the boot that will be useful.'

Cat parked the car in a little layby on the side of the road, but in truth, as she got out, she wondered just how many people would pass by. This wasn't the main road coasting along to Fionnphort. Rather, this was a side road that went off into the fields and she was struggling to see many houses around. 'Okay, Tiff. How are we going to get close then?'

Tiff was at the rear of the car opening the boot and, as she unzipped her bag, she began to pull a dark green patchy cloth out into the sunlight. Cat soon realised the cloth was more of a blanket with holes in it. It looked military, like something a sniper would wear over them if they were hiding in the bushes.

'Where'd you get that?'

'Well, now I'm becoming a detective,' said Tiff, 'I felt I needed something just in case we had to stake somewhere out so I bought it in a shop. It's quite good, isn't it? It'll probably fit the two of us.'

'But how are we getting from here, over to there and what

are we going to do? Just sit and watch the house all day?'

'That's exactly what I intend to do,' said Tiff. 'Plop myself down and watch what goes on. You said that's the house where the man is.'

'Okay, let's get on with it then,' said Cat and reached inside her jeans pocket, pulling out a hair tie. After fixing her hair up, she helped Tiff carry the blanket across and they climbed over a fence into a field.

'Down low,' said Tiff. 'Keep down low as we go across.' Slowly, they crossed the field, bent over until they reached the other side and only one field stood between them and the house in question.

'Now we throw this over us,' said Tiff. 'Remember, keep it quiet. I'll use hand signals.'

'You can just whisper in my ear,' said Catriona. 'I'm not going to see hand signals with this thing over us, am I?'

'Good idea, but I'll have to be quiet.'

With that, Tiff began to pull the blanket over the top of both of them. Catriona fought to get some holes that she could see out of. Once Cat held a big thumbs-up close to her niece, the pair started to slowly make their way across the field before them. Catriona was glad she was wearing sturdy boots but, as they eventually knelt down in the field, she felt the wet sink into the knees of her jeans. She was also beginning to realise that, if the weather turned bad, she was basically under a holey blanket in just a jumper and would soon get cold. Maybe this hadn't been the best idea after all.

'Do you have any binoculars?' asked Cat. Beside her, Tiff reached into a small bag she was carrying and pulled small binoculars up to her face and began looking towards the house.

'Can you see anything?'

'Shh. I'm watching. I will signal for you if I need to talk to you.'

Cat felt the wet continue to work up her knees into her thighs. It was cold and all she wanted to do was to keep her legs moving. Unfortunately, this was the last thing that could happen under the blanket, she reckoned. If it started moving uncontrollably, it would be more easily seen.

'There's somebody in there,' said Tiff. 'It's not easy to see but there's the occasional shadow moving about.'

'Are you sure?' asked Cat. 'You're not just making this up? Bits and pieces going across the front of your binoculars?'

'No, I know what I'm doing. Trust me. There's somebody in that house.'

'So how do we get to it? Do we knock on the door, just bang on it and hope that somebody arrives and says, "Yes, come in? By the way, my name's Matthias."'

'No,' said Tiff. 'We could go up and knock it.'

'As what exactly?' asked Cat. 'What are we going to knock the door as?'

It was then the sound of a car engine could be heard coming gradually closer, increasing in intensity. They saw a red van pull up in front of the house. A young postman got out and rapped the door hard. After knocking the door several times, Cat watched the man try to push the door open but it was locked. Shaking his head, he took his small package and put it back inside the van, before driving off.

'Somebody is in that house, Tiff, but they're making a good job of pretending they're not. After all, they didn't want their post.'

'Well, maybe going up now is not the best idea,' said Tiff. 'We should try and approach at night, sneak in undetected.'

'I suppose you're going to tell me you've got a whole load of secret lock picks to open the door with.'

'No. Not a whole load. I do have a few ideas though.'

4

Chapter 04

Tiff had wanted the pair to stay together watching the house until nightfall, but Catriona's stomach was getting the better of her so instead, she left her niece covered up while she drove off to the nearest village to find something to eat. By the time she'd parked up in the lay-by again, Tiff had made her way back over to the car. She had an assortment of snacks sitting on the dashboard of the car.

'If we sit here, we can see if anybody leaves the house with a car,' advised Cat. 'I doubt somebody's going to go off on foot.'

'Not if they're hiding out here. I mean, where do they go? There's nowhere around this building.'

'You didn't seem to get very much grub,' said Tiff. 'There's not a lot here I like.'

'Tiff, there wasn't a lot to choose from. I had to grab what was there. It was only a small shop, so if you don't like it, tough. This is what we're having.'

Catriona looked at the corned beef tin she was opening in her hands. 'Like I said, it's not much, but it'll do until we get something proper to eat.'

'Have you got something black in your case?' asked Tiff.

'I've got that big black baggy jumper,' said Catriona. 'Why?'

'You're going to need black jeans too. Blue shows up pretty well. Black's what we need. We're going in at night. We need to make sure they can't see us. I've got a couple of balaclavas.'

'Why are you carrying balaclavas?' asked Cat.

'Because as detectives, you never know when you have to break into somewhere.'

'You know we're not detectives. We're not some sort of law enforcement agency here. We're out on a limb with this, Tiff. I'm only doing it because they sullied Luigi's name.'

'Fair enough, but do you have any black jeans?'

'No.'

'They'll have to do, then. Probably best if we park the car somewhere else, though. It's a bit obvious sat here on the road. Maybe we can put it beside some barn or something and people will think it's just there for a good reason.'

Catriona nodded and drove the car further up the lane before pulling into a barn situated on the side. There was extraordinarily little around it, certainly no farmhouse. Having parked up, she went to the back of the car and changed into her black baggy jumper and took her balaclava from Tiff. Her niece, on the other hand, was dressed head to foot in black. As the sun had not yet died away and the evening still had some time to go, Cat thought her niece looked like the proverbial thief. The only thing she was missing was a swag bag over the back of her shoulder. Together the pair slowly walked down the road they'd come along until they got to where they'd parked the car earlier.

There was still no one about and as they made their way into the field and then covered themselves up with the camouflage blanket, they sneaked along, closer to the house. During the next three hours, as they waited for darkness to fall, Catriona found this time that the wet ground was soaking in through her jeans from the rear. Her bottom started to get cold and she wrapped herself up tight as best as she could. The day was by no means a wild one but sitting around in this muddy patch was not doing her any good.

As darkness finally fell, Tiff moved the blanket back off her head, leaving Catriona under it. Cat pushed it back off herself and watched as Tiff stared with the binoculars.

'What can you see?'

'Shush. Don't raise your voice. I think he may have gone to bed. What time is it, anyway?'

Cat checked her watch, briefly illuminating a light before switching it off again. 'Just gone midnight.'

'Right. Let's make a move,' said Tiff. Together the women sneaked along the edge of the field, went through a bush, and then started to make their way up the driveway towards the house. It was only when they'd reached that Cat thought about the idea that there may have been alarms or trips going off, but as nobody seemed to be reacting, she thought it best to continue.

'I think there're bedrooms at the back of the house,' said Tiff. 'Come on. We're clearly going in through the front door.'

'How do you know it's not alarmed?' asked Cat, and with that Tiff quickly looked around one side of the house before walking back and looking around the other.

'There's no alarm on the outside. That's what they do, isn't it? They put alarms on the outside.'

'Well, you're the master thief. You tell me.' Tiff shook

her head, pulling the balaclava down firmly over her face. Catriona found that the eye holes were not comfortable, her eyelashes striking against them, causing her to blink through the darkness, but she saw Tiff take out a small leather wallet, open it and remove some picks with which to attack the door before her. Cat was impressed as the girl worked quickly and the door suddenly flew open.

'Nice one. Now let's get inside quickly.'

Tiff stepped forward, slowly moving around the hallway. It was hard to see in the dark, but at the far end there seemed to be some sort of stool and possibly a phone attached to the wall. There were stairs that led up and Cat thought it best not to go along these quite yet. Instead, the pair made their way along the hall and ended up in the kitchen at the rear of the building. Tiff started to shift through letters that were lying on the table but quickly realised she couldn't see. Removing a penlight from her back pocket, she peered at them. 'These look like old bills.'

Cat made her way along the kitchen, starting to open cupboards. At first, she was careful but realising there wasn't a lot here except for kitchenware and pots and pans, Catriona became quicker, checking drawers at a rate of knots, but she truly couldn't see inside them for any great length of time. And then she pulled open a top one, realising too late that the catches that would stop it from coming out too far were not there. The drawer dropped, her hand still hanging on to the handle and a mass of cutlery clattered onto the floor.

'Nice one,' said Tiff. 'He's bound to hear that.'

'Shh,' said Cat. 'We might get away with it if he's asleep. He might not have heard it.'

'The dead would hear that,' said Tiff. 'Come on. We should

get out of here.'

'No,' said Cat. 'Don't move. I can't hear him yet.' With that, she froze in the spot, cocking her head to one side to indicate she was listening. Tiff shook her head, but she waited also. At first, there was nothing and then the sudden click of a switch. The lights in the hall came on and someone slowly made their way down the stairs.

'Bugger,' said Cat. 'Let's get going. Come on,' and made for the rear door, but in the darkness, she found it locked. The footsteps could be heard descending the stairs, making their way out to the hall. But then in the distance Cat heard cars. There was a screech as they pulled up on the driveway side of the house and then came a rap on the door. Cat grabbed Tiff and pulled her towards her as a man entered the kitchen at full pace, knocked them both flying onto the floor and began to unlock the back door.

'Who's that?' said Tiff.

'A man in trouble,' said Cat, grabbing her niece and pulling her away into the dining room. The back door flung open, the man escaped, racing as hard as he could, and then came a crash indicating the front door had been taken off its hinges. Cat hauled Tiff, pulling her down underneath the dining table and they watched as several sets of legs ran through the kitchen and then out of the back door.

'There he goes,' came a shout amidst a large number of curses and swears. Tiff tried to stand up but Cat pull her down again, holding tight.

'Ride this out,' she said. 'Just ride it out. No need to be afraid.'

'I'm not afraid; I want to go after them,' said Tiff.

'Don't move,' whispered Cat. 'Don't move, stay put.' It was two minutes later when Catriona decided that no one was in the house. She made her way to the back door and looked out. She had to throw herself back into the house as someone ran past the door but he didn't come in and soon she heard cars from the front of the house disappearing. Grabbing Tiff, Cat made her way out of the rear door, ran to the back of the house and the two women began to route across the field and then back up towards their own car, still stationed outside the barn. As they calmly drove back down the road, they saw the last of the cars leaving the house possibly a good way behind the earlier departures who had been in pursuit of the man.

'Best to follow them,' said Tiff. 'We can find out where they're going, where he's going.'

'How am I going to do that? It's the middle of the night and we're driving alone. They're going to see our headlights wondering who's behind them.'

Tiff reached over and switched off the headlights.

'Don't worry, you'll see their lights ahead. Just follow them. Keep a reasonable distance.'

'You're not the one driving,' said Cat, 'I am. This is my licence.'

'No,' said Tiff. 'These are the people besmirching Luigi's name, that's what you said. You said you wanted to sort it. Let's get going.'

Cat only shook her head, reached up and pulled the balaclava off and threw it into the backseat. 'Keep an eye out for me. Just tell me if I clip anything,' said Cat as the front wheel rolled the curb before bouncing back down again.

'You mean like that one?' said Tiff.

'Just do it, okay? That's all I ask, is you just do it.'

Cat was expecting a fast chase ending up in a car burning in a ditch somewhere, but instead she found that the car ahead was driving at a reasonably sedate pace which seemed to follow the long road back towards Craignure. Having reached there, the car pulled over to one side. Cat stopped some distance away still with her lights off and waited. Maybe someone had spotted the man, maybe they hadn't. Surely this car would have been in mobile phone contact with the pursuers. Either way, there was no way the women could know where this other man was. For ten minutes the car sat motionless, and Catriona began to drum her fingers on the steering wheel. She wasn't in control of this, wasn't in charge of what was happening but if that was Matheus Warner who these people were after, she had to find him and ask him what was going on? Why were they after him? Surely this was the man who had taken her jewellery, for why would he have such pursuers.

The car pulled away again and Catriona, still with her lights off, tailed it from some distance back. As he drove along, Catriona realised they were coming close to Glenforsa airfield, the small airport that was used for the island. On reaching Glenforsa, the car ahead pulled over to one side, causing Cat to drive off the road again and hide out. She could see the entrance to the airfield and saw two cars driving out of it. They seemed to be blocking the gate at the entrance and then a loud crack of gunfire ripped through the night. A single car drove from the centre of the airfield beside the hangar all the way out to the exit and then the four cars drove off together.

'What was that? That was gunfire, Tiff. You think they've shot him? What's happened?'

'I don't know,' said Tiff, 'but they hopefully haven't got him. If they do, we can't get him if he's in those cars but maybe he's over in the airfield. After all, why shoot him there making all that noise and then drive off with him. Maybe he hid out, maybe he shot at them. We should go and look.'

Cat thought about this. The women were unarmed, so they were either walking up to somebody with a gun or somebody who may have been shot by one. It all seemed a bit hairy but whatever, somebody knew what was happening with Luigi's name. Somebody knew what her husband was or wasn't and she needed to know too. Cat put her foot down, drove the car back onto the road and dropped Tiff at the gate of the airfield. She then spun the car around and parked it just up from the airfield before running back towards the airfield gates. As she hurried along the small road up towards the hangars, she heard Tiff tell her to have a look towards the building ahead of her. There were not many buildings, but there were a few hangars and Cat ran over, trying the door of an administration block. It was locked. She made her way to the next hangar, again, finding it closed and she wasn't able to open it. But then there was another small one and she saw Tiff gently pulling back the door. She slipped inside and Catriona followed her.

'Are you able to smell gun smoke in the air?'

Catriona didn't know what Tiff was on about. She couldn't smell anything. As she stepped inside, she saw Tiff standing there with a small penlight focusing on the floor. Cat followed the beam with her eye and saw a head lying on the floor. Coming close to Tiff, she watched as her niece ran the light along the body of a well-dressed man. He had a suit on, shirt, tie as well, along with black shoes. Was this the man who had run from the house? Well, there was mud on the shoes, and as the torch panned along his legs, Cat could see the trousers had been pulled, little threads tugged at, as if the man had gone through a thickened hedge.

Tiff bent down, placing her hand beside the man's neck.

'There's no pulse. I can't feel a pulse.' Carefully, she swept her small torch over the man again.

'Don't touch him,' said Cat. 'Don't touch him.' On the air, she heard the sirens of a police car. 'Come on,' she cried. 'Let's go.'

'Wait,' said Tiff. She was delicately lifting up the jacket of the man. The pen torch shined on a white shirt, which was now covered in a bloody red stain. 'They shot him,' said Tiff. 'They bloody well shot him.'

5

Chapter 05

'That's a dead body. We need to get out of here,' scolded Cat. 'We can't hang around. You can hear the sirens.'

'Just a moment. This might be the only chance we get.'

'Tiff, we're not messing about here. That's a dead body; he's been shot and we're standing here. Let's go.'

Tiff turned with a serious air and stared at her aunt. 'You were the one who said you wanted to clear Luigi's name. You have to take these risks. You have to be on top of things. It's not a problem—I'm on top of it.' With that, Tiff pulled out a pair of disposable gloves, snapping them on over hands.

'Tiff, it's not playtime. Come on, let's get moving.'

'Just a moment.' Tiff knelt down and reached inside the jacket of the man on the floor. She instantly searched inside before pulling out a brown envelope. 'This looks interesting.'

'Interesting or not, those sirens are getting closer,' said Cat. 'You could always move the car.'

'The car is out of the way, don't worry about the car. We

need to be like the car. We need to be out of the way. Do you understand me? Now, let's get a move on, Tiff.'

Tiff ignored her aunt, opening up the brown envelope and removing a small white wallet. Inside were plane tickets.

'Look at this, Cat. It's return tickets. He has return tickets to Denmark. I'm just going to put it down and photograph it. It looks like he was getting out of here. In fact, there's a pair of tickets here, or there should be. According to the documentation, this is for two, two people to go to Denmark. Somebody's already taken one and gone. Maybe they've got the cobra's fang.'

'Or maybe we're going to get lifted for murder. Hurry up.'

Tiff did anything but rush as she carefully placed the tickets on the ground, taking a photograph of them with her mobile phone before delicately inserting them back in the envelope and placing the envelope inside the man's jacket.

'There's one thing that's strange, though. It's only got a lead passenger's name here. And that lead passenger is Mathias Weiner. Well, that's your thief, isn't it?' said Tiff. 'That's him right there. It doesn't have the name of who was travelling with him. I'll just see if there's anything else on him.'

'Come on,' said Cat, moving to the door of the hangar and looking out. The sirens were getting closer but they were still somewhere in the distance. That was the thing about Mull. It was quiet, especially out here on the airstrip with nothing about. The only thing you could hear was the occasional lap of water over from the sound of Mull where you could see lights of passing vessels. Otherwise, all was quiet at this time of night.

'Yes, this is Mathias, Tiff. I've checked his wallet. It says so, Mathias Weiner. I'll just take some photographs of this.'

Cat looked out from the hangar. In the darkness of the night she could see blue lights flashing coming ever closer and realised that they were now nearby.

'We need to move and get off this airfield,' said Cat. 'We can't hang about. Put it all back, Tiff, all back and let's go.'

'Okay, but we can't rush. We don't want people to know we've been here.'

'Tiff, if we don't rush, people won't need to know we've been here—we'll be here; they'll walk in on us. Hurry.'

'You need to take a calm attitude to this,' said Tiff. 'You are dealing with an expert.'

'Expert? You've read a couple of books. How are you an expert?'

'Two cases done so far. I'm an expert. A lot of people don't solve things like that in their lifetime.'

Catriona shook her head. This girl would be the death of her. She ran over, grabbed Tiff's arm and started to pull her towards the door.

'I haven't got the envelope back in his jacket yet. I'm with you, just give me thirty seconds.'

Catriona ran back to the door and glanced out. 'We haven't got thirty seconds, come on.'

'Don't go out the front anyway,' said Tiff. 'Let's go out the back of the hangar. They'll come racing into the open doors at the front. They're not going to go to the back, are they?'

Sometimes Catriona hated to admit that Tiff was actually more switched on than she was. In the heat of the moment, she could see the situation. Sometimes she made some particularly good decisions.

'Okay, out we go.' Together the women ran towards the back of the hangar and Tiff pointed to a door that led into a corridor.

At the end of the corridor, Cat could see the bar of fire exit and ran forward, pushing it hard, opening the door.

'We're meant to be quiet going about,' said Tiff. 'Sneaking.'

'We're not sneaking anywhere. They're about to hit this place. Get out.'

Tiff delicately closed the fire door behind her making sure it was shut properly. Cat was desperate to get moving in a quicker fashion, but she knew any interjection now would just generate more procrastination from Tiff. The best was to let her niece just get on with it.

Cat turned and looked at the surrounding field, making her way into the grass. It was reasonably long, about knee height, and crouching down in her black gear she wondered if anyone would be able to see her. The rain started just as Tiff joined her and Catriona cursed. This was not her idea of fun. Carefully, they made their way over to the surrounding perimeter fence, which thankfully was not that high, unlike most large airfields. At the larger airports, even if you had a chance to get over any of the perimeter fencing, it was lit up. Here on this small island airfield, it was more a fence to keep sheep out, small animals rather than any would-be perpetrator of a nefarious action. Together, they climbed over the barbed wire fence, carefully placing their feet between the barbs before jumping over to the far side. They made their way quickly to where Cat had left the car at the side of the road, driving off in the opposite direction to which they'd come from.

'We need to go and get changed,' said Cat.

'I'd love to get back inside that house, 'said Tiff. 'I bet he's hidden some stuff away. We might be able to find out who else is involved with him or where he was going in Denmark. We haven't really got much at the moment from having searched his body. If we don't find anything else, the trail's going to be cold.'

'We got out before the police arrived. I'd rather the trail be cold than we end up in a cell. Let's just find a lay-by somewhere and get changed out of this black stuff. We look well dodgy.'

'Okay,' said Tiff, 'but then we turn around and go the other way. We need to get back to that house. It's not so late that the idea of us travelling past is going to look suspicious. After all, our bed and breakfast is down that way. If I drive and we stop in somewhere for a couple of drinks or whatever, you'd smell right if we get stopped. I'm a teetotaller, so it'll just be me driving my aunt back.'

'Oh, so you want me to play the pissed-up fool, do you?'

'That's about right,' said Tiff. 'I think you can manage that.'

Cat was about to get angry until she realised what Tiff was doing. The ploy was right, the delivery and coaxing of her partner was extremely wrong but her niece had the right idea.

The women continued up the road until they reached Tobermory where they found a pub still open. Once inside Catriona knocked back a couple of double whiskeys and they left five minutes later, happy that the smell of alcohol was on her breath. With their black garb safely stored in the boot where the spare tyre was, the women drove back along the road, past the airport. There was a small police operation in progress, stopping cars passing by and Tiff slowed to a halt as a torch light indicated she should stop. She wound the window down and a young officer placed his head inside.

'Sorry to disturb you, ma'am, miss, but I'd like to ask you some questions. Have you been around here earlier on tonight?'

'Oh, we passed this way,' said Tiff. 'I was just taking my aunt up to Tobermory. She's had a few drinks so I'm just taking her safely back to the B&B. We're just over on a bit of a holiday.'

'Okay,' said the officer, leaning in and suddenly getting the smell of alcohol off Catriona's breath. 'Did you see anything when you went past around the airfield at all?'

'I don't think so,' said Tiff. 'I mean, it's just an airfield, isn't it? There's a lot of police cars about though.'

'Unfortunately, there's been an incident, but nothing for you to worry about. If you just want to continue on, it won't be a problem.'

Tiff wound up the window and quietly drove on while Catriona pulled down the vanity mirror and looked out through the rear of the car to see more vehicles being stopped.

'Do you think it's a good idea to go to the man's house? Will they not be there yet?'

'This is the island police. By the time they find out who he is and they get somebody else round in the car, it could be another few hours, I would reckon,' said Tiff. 'So, if we wait, there's no chance of searching the house. If we get there now, we could do it before anybody else arrives.'

'There was nothing else on those tickets, nowhere to trace where in Denmark anyone was going?'

'No, said Tiff, 'Nothing. We need to find out what's going on. We need to get some way of tracing your jewellery. I mean, you still want to clear Luigi's name?'

Cat flashed a look at Tiff. Of course, she did, but things were just getting a little serious. 'Okay, let's do it,' said Catriona and sat back in her seat while Tiff drove the car towards the house they'd been at earlier. Parking it up about a quarter of a mile away in the drive of a house to allay any suspicion, the women got out and changed again into their black outfits. The rain was still pouring down. Catriona felt cold as she made her way across fields behind Tiff. As they approached the house, her niece turned around, handed her a pair of disposable gloves and Catriona snapped them on. She pulled the balaclava tighter around her head and watched closely for any signs of movement in the house. There were none but the back door was open, still swinging, and together, the pair slowly made their way around the driveway, carefully stepping across the stony drive, so as to make as little sound as possible. Stepping inside the rear door, Catriona saw a house that was dark and pulled out a penlight from her outfit. Tiff instructed her to make sure she pointed it down until they were well inside. Catriona stepped past some spilt cereal, maybe a victim when the man was chased from his house.

'What are you hiding, Mathias?' said Tiff under her breath. 'Where is it?' Together the women walked along the corridor and turned into a front lounge. They opened up cupboards of a sideboard, looked through magazine racks, but there was nothing. Next, they made their way into a small bedroom which looked like it hadn't been slept in and found nothing in a wardrobe. Again, they continued on into the room behind, this time a larger bedroom with a double bed that looked like it had been slept in recently.

In the wardrobe hung a few jackets. Cat carefully searched through them but found nothing. There were trousers too, a couple of shirts and T-shirts in a drawer. It was like the man was on holiday, a small amount of clothing which he'd clearly had to leave behind when the others had come for him.

'This is hopeless, Tiff,' said Catriona. 'I mean we're going through all this stuff but there's nothing left behind. He's not going to leave it lying for people, is he?' Catriona stepped back from the wardrobe she was currently searching, then found herself stumbling across a rug on the bedroom floor. 'Oh, that's a bit of a dip,' she said. 'That's the problem with old places, they never sort out the floors; everything always goes after a number of years. You get a rickety plank and that, you don't bother pulling it up as they want it to look natural, look old. That's not good when the place is falling apart, though, is it?'

Tiff was turning around shining a light where Catriona stood. 'That's interesting,' said Tiff.

'No, it's not. It's just bad workmanship; need to sort themselves out, get it fixed if people are staying in a home like this.'

Tiff pulled back the rug on the floor and Catriona stood on the floorboard which creaked. Taking a small knife from her pocket, Tiff slid it down the side of the floorboard before prising it upwards.

'The nails in this are very loose. This has been lifted before,' said Tiff.

'It doesn't look like it.'

'Oh, it is,' countered Tiff, prising even harder as the floorboard flipped up and Tiff moved it to one side. She looked in, scanning with her torch and Catriona tried to see past Tiff's head to see if she could find anything. 'Can't see anything, I can almost touch the floor though,' said Tiff. 'Put your arm in; yours are longer than mine; see what you can find.'

Catriona looked at the black space beneath the torchlight. 'Oh,' she said, 'there could be anything down there. Rats, spiders.'

'Yes,' said Tiff, 'but he might have stored something down there. Put your hand in and have a feel around.'

Catriona rolled up her sleeve, not happy about what she was

about to do, got down her knees, and then reached inside the small gap with her hand. Her fingers felt a cold damp concrete floor. When she walked her hand along, something touched it. Catriona whipped her hand back out. There was something down there.

'That's probably a rat or a mouse or something. They've got to walk around in the dark, don't they? See if there's anything else down there.'

'What do you mean "see if there's anything else down there"? Something's alive.'

'Stop it. You've got the long arms, just put them down. Stop being a baby about it,' said Tiff.

'I'm not being a baby, but rats can bite. I'd have to go to the hospital and get an injection. You've heard of rabies, I take it.'

'You don't need to worry about rabies here, we're on the Isle of Mull. Put your hand down.' Catriona cast a look at Tiff. 'Do it for Luigi; come on—he needs you.'

Catriona grimaced. When did Tiff learn to play people like that? When did she learn how to take their emotions and use them against them? Catriona shook her head before leaning down and placing her hand into the gap again. Cautiously, she walked her hand around the floor, feeling the cold shell of the concrete on her bare fingers. She walked left and right as far as she could, anticipating something biting her hand any minute, and then her hand touched something.

'Oh, something there.'

'What?' said Tiff.

Catriona moved her hand again. It was still there, but it felt like plastic. Her hand continued and felt more of the plastic and she began to try to pull the object towards her, it was thin and she realised it was some sort of wallet for documents.

She grabbed the wallet and pulled her arm up, placing it on the floor. Tiff bent over with a flashlight, popping the plastic button, and checked the documents inside. Just then, a blue light lit up the house from outside. It flashed, casting indistinct shadows around the room.

'Quick,' said Tiff, and pushed the floorboard back down, dragging the rug across it. 'Out the kitchen,' she said. 'We need to go.'

Catriona did not wait; instead, making her way back along the hall to the kitchen at the rear, she then delicately tried to cross the stones onto the grass. She got a glance over her shoulder and saw Tiff delicately closing the door. *She shouldn't have done that*, thought Cat. *The door was open previously. Oh well, too late, time to go.* Together, the pair raced across the darkness at the rear of the house, occasionally lit up by a blue light. When they made it to the road, they were able to look back and saw two police cars. There was some activity around the house, torches being shone. Arriving back at the car, the pair took off their blacks before getting inside it.

'What do we do?'

'Back to the B&B,' said Cat. 'We need to get back to the B&B, have a look at these documents, see if they mean anything.'

Tiff started the car and drove away from the house where they had parked, up a small track, exploring it to see where it would end up. Thankfully, it turned back on itself and came to the main road again and the pair breathed a sigh of relief. The hour was late when they made it inside their bed and breakfast. Fortunately, they had been furnished with the key and did their best not to wake anyone up. On entering the room, Tiff immediately put the document down and started going through it but Cat felt a sudden urge going through her;

she was nervous, shaking. It was not the body—she had seen one before, but this man had been shot and it was to do with Luigi's jewellery.

'Going for a shower,' said Catriona. 'You have a look at that. I can wait, and you can tell me what it is.' Tiff simply nodded. Cat realised that the document was the only thing that mattered now. Tiff couldn't see Catriona was shaking, couldn't see the nervousness welling up inside her, as well as the wonder and worry about what Luigi was really involved with. As she stood beneath the shower, she wanted the warm water to wash it all away, but it didn't. Had her man been a thief? Surely not. He couldn't have hidden that from her. What else didn't she know about him?

6

Chapter 06

When Catriona emerged from the shower, she could hear Tiff chattering to herself in excited tones next door. Wrapping a towel around her, she made her way into the twin bedroom and saw a number of documents set out on one of the beds. There were thin, intricate diagrams on several of the pieces of paper. Catriona's eyes widened as she saw the scale of documents in front of her.

'There must be nearly 30 pages in here. Tiff, what are they?'

'This is how to rob an Italian bank,' said Tiff. 'At least as far as I can tell. It's not all here. It's bits and pieces, but it's definitely plans for robbing a bank.' Tiff held up a piece of paper. 'This one's a schematic; it's hand-drawn as well, or probably traced over, because the paper is very, very thin. It was done back in the day when they didn't have a lot of computers. Looks like a classy job, though, as far as I can tell.'

'What do you know about breaking into banks?'

'Well, I certainly wouldn't write it all down and store it under the floorboard. Certainly, once I'd done it. This is how many years later? I'm not quite sure why we have this, or why he had it. Maybe he was extorting them. Maybe he was running a scheme to get them to cough up more money. I don't know.'

'Have you been able to put it all together, though?' asked Catriona. 'I mean, does it read from one place to the other? Is it just a series of notes? Are they random?'

'Oh, there's a thought process to it. I mean, the pages aren't numbered, I've been trying to put them into an order,' said Tiff. She grabbed another piece of paper and slid it past one that was on the bed. 'These ones over here are very much about the robbery, but over here, talk about distribution, and who to go to, contacts, but a lot of the contacts seem to be in code. Also, a lot of the writing is in Italian. My Italian's not the best.'

'Your Italian is non-existent,' said Cat, 'Give it to me.' Though Catriona was not fluent in Italian, she had learned enough from Luigi to be able to make herself passable in the street, or indeed, in the lawyer's office where she spent a considerable time after his funeral. 'This is all about dividing up,' said Catriona, looking at a piece of paper. 'It's talking about where they're going to put it. Although it's unusual because it refers to the prize and it's in plural, it's not in the singular. I don't know, is a cobra's fang something you would look at plurally? I reckon you could do. Maybe they're going to break it up into different pieces. There's definitely the mention of a cobra in here, so, I guess it was the fang they were after. Maybe they were a pair. Maybe they were cobra's fangs. Maybe Luigi didn't know that. Is there any mention of Luigi's name?'

Tiff shook her head and smiled at her aunt. 'It doesn't seem to be. There's nothing here indicating he was involved.'

'Well, he was not involved then,' said Catriona. 'Are there any names? Is there anywhere for us to go from this? Because from what I can see, we have a lot of plans attached to nobody, and if they don't attach to nobody, they can still attach them to Luigi, if they suspect him.'

'Nothing that I've seen yet. Although there are a couple of pages over there, the writing is so dense, and it's all in Italian. I can't tell what they are.'

Catriona sat down on a chair in the corner of the room. 'Bring those over to me. Let me take a look at them.' Tiff brought the pages over to Catriona, and she pointed towards the kettle so that her niece would make a cup, but Tiff just shrugged her shoulders. 'What?' she asked.

'Tea? Hot drink? Something,' said Catriona.

'Don't you know how to make it?' asked Tiff.

'Reading all the documents, trying to work out what's going on? Maybe you could kindly make the tea.'

'Do you have tea?' said Tiff.

'Yes,' said Catriona, and then ignored her niece, putting her head down and concentrating on the paper before her. The writing was indeed dense and written in cursive script, so Catriona had to concentrate hard on what was being written. She was better with spoken Italian than she ever was with written, and it was taking her some time going through it bit by bit, finger pointing at word after word, breaking down what was being said. Her excitement grew as she realised she was looking at possible locations that the goods were going to be passed off to. However, she was quite surprised when she saw the number of different countries that the items were bound for.

'Denmark, Tiff. That ticket said Denmark, didn't it?'

'Yes,' said Tiff. 'Definitely Denmark, and one ticket gone already. Mathias never made it.'

'No, he didn't, but he went to Denmark. We might need to go to Denmark.'

'Well, that's probably where we're going, anyway,' said Tiff. 'After all, that's the only lead we've got.'

'I don't know. This is talking about goods being split up, going into different places. At the moment, I can see Denmark. I can also see a number of other ones, countries that they've gone to.'

'Where else is there?'

'Well, there's a place in Luxembourg, for a start, and then there's also Liechtenstein, and also, as far as I can tell, appears to be one in Belgium, Bruges, although that doesn't look like a house address. There're also names with it. Four names for four houses,' said Cat. 'Clemson, that's the Copenhagen one. I've got a Mertens in Belgium. I've got a Jones in Luxembourg. That's a bit bizarre. Surely that's an alias,' said Cat.

'What about the other one, Liechtenstein? What's in Liecht-enstein?'

'Weiss, it just says Weiss.'

'There're only surnames as well,' said Tiff. 'Well, at least that's something. These might have been the people who did the robbery. They may just be the fences, the people they're going through to get rid of their jewellery. I mean, we don't even know what was fully taken, do we? We just know it was from an Italian bank. We haven't got a lot of details.'

'I doubt we're going to get a lot of details because the police are not going to talk to me,' said Cat. 'Not in a nice way, anyway. They'll probably suspect that I'm hiding something, or I've got Luigi's side of the loot, but I haven't. They took it from me. We need to get it back.'

Catriona stood up and walked over to the window of the bed

and breakfast. She pulled back the curtains and looked out into the night. There were a few lights around but mainly it was just dark. As she stared, she saw the odd shadow and her heart skipped a beat. *Mathias Weiner was killed for whatever he knew about the cobra's fang. Somebody was too ready to just get rid of the man. Should Catriona race after this, what risk was she putting her niece into? This wasn't some nice little play murder mystery that she could tag along on. The people that did this clearly meant business and they obviously were too happy to just kill someone.*

'I think we put it away now, Tiff,' said Catriona. 'Wrap it up and we'll talk about this in the morning. That's probably the best thing to do.'

'Right now, I think we should look through the rest of it, see what else we can come up with. I mean, we've got four places now. Four places to go and look at.'

'Bedtime, it's getting late. We could both do with the sleep. Come on, Tiff, pack it all up. Put it back in the wallet; then it's there ready for tomorrow.'

Catriona slipped out of her dressing gown and put on her pyjamas. She watched as Tiff folded up the pieces of paper, put them away on the dressing table, and then made her way over to her own bed. It took ten minutes before Tiff had undressed, put her earphones in and then Catriona could hear her snoring.

There was no way Catriona could take Tiff through all this. These men could be brutal, could just finish you off if you got caught out. She'd have to do this one alone. Her brother would never forgive her if she lost her niece, not over something like this. This was her fight. It was Luigi's name that was besmirched, no one else's. It wasn't her own family. Catriona would do this.

After an hour of lying perfectly still and making sure that

Tiff was asleep, Catriona slowly rolled out of bed. She took her small bag, packed up what clothes she had, all in the dark and hoped she wouldn't forget anything. Placing a hand inside one of the zip pockets, she felt for her passport. She'd need to go and she needed to be smart; otherwise, Tiff would follow her. Other people could follow her too. She'd take cash out, pay for everything that way, that would be easier. Nobody could trace her cards then, know where she was going. Or there was the other account she had; the secret one Luigi had always kept for her. It had not seemed strange at the time but now, although useful, it did appear strange.

Turning around, Catriona stared at her niece lying fast asleep. The eyes didn't move, her chest rose and fell gently. She hoped Tiff would forgive her, but she was doing this in part out of Tiff's own interest. The girl could get so involved and she never really saw the danger. This was for the better. Catriona picked up her bag and began walking for the door. She opened it slowly and nearly cursed as the light from the lit hallway shone into the bedroom. She quickly turned around and looked at Tiff. No, she was still asleep. Still that same slow motion of her chest rising and falling underneath her covers. Catriona would go on her own. She alone would set out to clear Luigi's name. Watching her niece, she placed her bag down, reached into her pocket, and tied her hair up behind her with a simple black tie. Having done that, she blew a kiss to her niece and turned to walk out the door.

'Where are you going?'

How on Earth is she awake? thought Catriona and then turned around quickly, staring at her niece. 'It's too dangerous. You need to stay. Your father would never forgive me to take you into this. I've got addresses. I'll talk to you. I'll write—you can advise me what to do.'

Tiff was out of bed in an instant. 'What do you mean? You can't go without me? I'm the brains of the outfit. You would get lost. You wouldn't have a clue what you're doing.'

'Excuse me, I know to handle myself. Remember, I'm the one who can sort people out. You would get lost amongst them.'

'But you wouldn't have a clue about what was going on. You wouldn't be able to see who had done what. I can track down these people. I know how to do it. I know how to go into places and not leave a mark.'

'Since when?'

'Since the house and the airport. I've read about this. I know what I'm doing. You need me with you. In fact, it's probably more that I need you with me.'

Catriona stopped in her tracks. Tiff was saying she needed her. This was a new development. Usually, Tiff was just taking Catriona along for the ride, or so she thought, never happy to admit that her aunt was looking after her. 'I can't do it, Tiff; it's too dangerous. There's a dead man at the airfield. If that happened to you—'

'If that happened to me—it won't happen to me. You know it won't because I'll be with you. I'll be covering it off and I'll have your back and you'll have mine. We're a team. You're like my sidekick.'

Catriona rolled her eyes inside. Sidekick, she actually believes that I'm her sidekick. 'No, it's too perilous; you need to stay.'

'You go and I'll tell my father where you've gone. You know he'll come after you. You know he wants to keep you safe. He'll not want the family in a scandal.'

'You're blackmailing me. How do you get off blackmailing

me? I'm family, I'm your aunt. I took you away on holidays. I took you with me when no one else would.'

'So, take me now. You know I'll be useful. You need someone to watch your back. You've got nobody out there.'

Catriona stood, shoulders now slumped, looking at the beaming face of her niece. The girl was serious; she really thought Catriona needed her. Really thought that she could solve all this. What would she do if she left her? Who knew who was coming after Catriona? These other individuals she could handle, but not the family, not the family trying to pull her back. Then they'd tell Luigi's family and they would probably get involved and they'll be rows and arguments between them. It wasn't the thought of nasty men that bothered her; it was the thought of the family inquisition. Family coming and checking her out, being the black sheep again. She could have that, or she could have Tiff along for the ride.

'You're on, but I call the shots all the way,' said Catriona.

'Of course, but obviously, you need to follow my advice,' said Tiff.

Catriona shook her head and undid her hair at the back. Slowly, she stripped off her clothes, pulled her pyjamas back on from out of the small bag she'd packed, and made her way underneath her own covers again. Soon the light was switched off, and the pair of them lay in the darkness in each of the twin beds.

'So where do we start?' asked Catriona.

'Denmark. We head to Denmark. After all, that's what the missing ticket was for.'

'Six o'clock up and gone, then,' said Catriona.

'Six? I wake up when I wake up.'

'Six o'clock, or I'll be gone.' There was a decided 'Humph'

before the snoring of Tiff took over again. Part of Catriona was pleased Tiff was coming with her. She could do with the company, and, yes, she could probably do with her brains. But something else inside her was scared. If this hadn't been for Luigi, she would definitely be heading in the opposite direction.

7

Chapter 07

The next morning Catriona was up at five and realised that she only had a few hours' sleep. She wondered if she should return to bed, but there was too much running through her head. The thought that she actually would go somewhere, the thought that she might even have a chance of tracking down these people who had besmirched Luigi's name, was driving her on, along with wanting to get off the Isle of Mull quickly. The police would be asking questions. Hopefully, her car hadn't been seen. Whenever they had driven past the airfield, it had seemed okay but the sooner they put distance between here and the man's body, the better.

Where would they go to fly to Denmark as well? Would they need to head south? They could pick up a flight maybe in Glasgow or Edinburgh. That was probably the best bet. Still, Tiff could work that out; she was good at that sort of thing. But she'd have to be careful. If she paid it with her credit card, there would be a trace. People could come after them. She would need to use the other card—the one Luigi gave her for emergencies.

Standing on the side of the bed, she reached down into her small purse and pulled out the card that had come to mind. Luigi originally said it was just in case of trouble, in case someone had come after the family. He never said why but he said they could not be traced back making it more awkward for people to follow them around. Cat hadn't thought anything of it. Even when the cobra's fang was taken and they were saying that Luigi was involved, putting him down as a thief, the card never came to mind. Only now had it become a strange item but one she needed to use to maintain her secrecy.

The family in Italy didn't even know about this card, and she'd always thought that was the reason why, so her and Luigi could disappear, always thought that was why he had his own separate account. She knew there was a lot of money sitting in this bank, quietly stashed away. And she thought of their secret little rendezvous for those quiet dates when he couldn't be observed.

Luigi just had such pressure on him from his family to marry well, and to say they were disappointed when he came up with Catriona was an understatement in the extreme. He tried to talk about how she was a Munroe and had clan heritage in Scotland but he knew it was a lie. Her father is just a wealthy businessman, nothing more, nothing less. She wasn't any form of Scottish royalty. He was the one who had taken her, picked her up off the streets, and made her into something special. As soon as he died, they kicked her back down there, but not without his money. The family weren't going to fight for him so she'd have to do it.

There was a yawn beside Catriona. 'What time's it?' said Tiff.

'Time for you to get up. We need to get going. Get on that phone of yours and find out where we can get a flight to Skagen. That's where the address in Denmark is. How well do you know Skagen?'

'Never heard of it,' said Tiff. 'I'll get us a flight to Denmark, then we can drive there. I take it you have a licence to be able to hire a car or something.'

'Yes, something like that,' said Catriona, 'but you're not driving.'

'Why not?' said Tiff.

'Because you don't have a special licence. I do.'

The card wasn't the only thing that Luigi had given her. She did indeed have a special licence. It was false. It showed her face, and yes, she looked a bit younger than she did now, but it was still valid. Italian licence, good for travelling throughout Europe with something to keep her life secret. Catriona was wondering now what they were keeping their life secret from. Luigi couldn't be like this. This would have been for her and him to be alone, to be separate. Not to cover up misdemeanours he had, not to cover up a penchant for thievery.

It was as they breakfasted that Tiff placed her phone in front of Catriona. They needed to get off the island and take a flight that evening to Denmark, landing in Copenhagen. From there they would drive to Skagen and it would probably be the next morning by the time they got there. Catriona handed her card over to Tiff telling her to book the flight with it and also some accommodation on the way to Skagen. The downside of Tiff coming along was the fact she'd have to use her normal passport because there wasn't a cover for her.

However, her name wasn't as well-known as Catriona's. It even had the title of Contessa on it, so her other passport of

Francesca Rossi seemed like a good option. They'd have to hope nobody was coming looking for Tiff.

Catriona made a call back to the family home explaining to her father that they had decided to head off for a week's skiing. Despite her father's protests that it wasn't really the season, she said that Tiff was so in the mood. Catriona didn't feel like she could say no. She had planned for Tiff's board and equipment to be sent to a hotel in the Alps. Calling ahead, the hotel would put the item into storage but at least it would give credence to her cover story.

The women took the ferry off the Isle of Mull later that morning, before making their way across to Edinburgh and catching the flight to Copenhagen. When they touched down it was late evening; the sky was going dark, but fortunately, they had only thirty miles to go before stopping in a roadside hotel for the next morning. When Catriona woke, she was relieved to find no messages on her phone. No family seeking her. Maybe the cover story of skiing had worked. The family was used to Catriona just disappearing and doing what she wanted.

As Catriona drove along the road out to Skagen she became aware she wasn't sure what she was going to find at the address. Did she simply walk up and bang on the door? How did she approach this? She thought she would ask her niece.

'We stake it out first,' said Tiff. 'Try and see who lives there. Check out the local phone directories, things like that. Anything we can find, and ultimately knock the door. Say we have a parcel for someone, believe that it was this address. We'll make something up, something as long as it looks plausible,' said Tiff.

Catriona was not convinced but decided instead to concentrate on driving as she made her way along the Danish roads towards Skagen. It wasn't an overly large town and Catriona thought to herself that, really, towns and cities don't change that much. They've all got a little piece of the country they're in but really, it's all domiciles. The particular address in Skagen where they were heading was in a rather affluent area, and the streets were immaculate.

She pulled up some distance short of the house and stared at it. A two-story affair with a balcony above the front door. The bell was relatively new, and Catriona thought that the place looked like a very private neighbourhood. Maybe they'd be spotted, but at least they were in a hire car, probably mistaken for some tourists who got lost, stuck in a residential part instead of looking for the sights and sounds of the local town.

The women arrived sometime just before lunch and spent the next two hours sitting watching the house. There was a car in the drive and an elderly gentleman came out once to attend to his garden. They watched him for an hour moving plants about, removing weeds from the soil. When he disappeared back inside, Tiff suggested he might be the man they're looking for.

'Clausen, it said Clausen. I think this one could be him.'

'On what basis?' asked Cat.

'Well, I'm looking up on the internet, and there's definitely a Clausen here. Look, if you go through, it says Clausen attached to that address. He's in the house so he must be him.'

'Well, why don't you get what's in the back so we can do our parcel then.'

Tiff nodded and picked up a wrapped-up parcel they had prepared that morning. There were only chocolates in it but at least there was an excuse to turn up at the door. As they got out of the car, an older woman emerged, dressed in a pink top and some white jeans. She came out with a pair of secateurs and started cutting a hedge before she was followed by the man. He stood politely beside her holding a bag. Catriona watched him stand like a puppy as the woman dropped cuttings into the bag, talking to the man on occasion. He seemed to say truly little. Catriona got the feeling that this wasn't the Clausen they were looking for.

'Come on,' she said to Tiff, 'I don't think this is it. Let's go and find out. Bring those chocolates.' Tiff opened the door, stepped out and the pair began to walk towards the house. The woman looked up at their arrival and then sent the man around the drive to meet them before they could reach her.

'Good afternoon,' said Catriona. 'Hi there. I'm looking for Clausen, Mr. Clausen. I'm sorry, we've just come from the UK and we've been asked to drop these by a friend. I think it's just some chocolates in there. Are you Mr. Clausen?'

The man shook his head. The woman shouted over something in Danish and the man shook his head back. 'My wife is asking who you are. Can I say?'

'My name is Francesca,' said Catriona, 'Mr. Clausen is a friend of one of our friends, and they knew we were coming to Denmark. We're just doing a little sightseeing but they said, 'Can you go to Skagen and drop these off?"

The man shook his head, 'We don't much care for Mr. Clausen. We've had a few people come up since, not of the nicest sort.'

'Really?' said Catriona, 'I wasn't aware of that. We don't know Mr. Clausen personally, that's why we're asking. They didn't even give us a photograph. They just gave us the address.'

'Well, he's not here,' said the man before turning and listening to his wife shouting something at him in Danish. 'Clausen,' said the man, 'they want Clausen.' This seemed to cause the woman to become irritated and she stormed around out of her garden, past the hedge, and down to Catriona and Tiff. At once, she began in Danish to berate the pair of them.

'I'm sorry to bother you,' said Catriona. 'Apologies, I don't speak Danish.'

'Where are you from?'

'UK,' said Catriona. 'We're from the UK. I'm Francesca, this is Tiff.'

'Well Miss Francesca and Miss Tiff, if you're friends of Mr. Clausen, I don't want to know. We have people come here asking to see him, wanting to be put into a business by him.'

'That's not us. We just came to drop this off. A friend asked us to give this to him.'

'What is in there?'

'I don't know,' said Catriona, 'I haven't seen.'

'If I was you,' said the woman, 'I would open that now and check. He likes to stick things up his nose, the drugs, the women, things like that.'

'Right,' said Cat, 'I didn't realise. Do you know where he is now?',

'No, he went back to Copenhagen. That's all I know. Not a nice man.'

'In what way?'

'He has those clubs. What's your English word for it? Women clubs?'

'Do you mean gentlemen's clubs?' asked Tiffany. The woman looked amused and turned to her husband who denied all knowledge of knowing what any of these clubs were. 'The clubs with the women and the boobies,' she said. 'That sort of club.'

'Gentlemen's club,' said Catriona, 'I understand.'

'He owns quite a few of them in Copenhagen. Maybe you ask for him there,' said the man. His wife looked at him as if he shouldn't know anything about any of this.

'I just know,' he said, 'Of course I've never been. I don't go to those sorts of things.'

His wife said something in Danish, turned on her heel, and walked off. The man turned to Catriona. 'I don't. Why is she upset? I don't go to these things.'

'He does own them? If we ask for him there, we'll find him, yes?' said Catriona.

'Yes, you will but don't do those things. They don't treat them well, the women. You don't want to be in there.'

'Well, thank you for your time,' said Catriona, 'Come on, Tiff, looks like we have chocolates in our van.' With that, the women walked back to their car and drove away back to Copenhagen.

'So that's that, is it?' said Tiff.

'No, it isn't,' said Catriona, 'Of course not but I wasn't going to tell those people we're about to go charging into gentlemen's clubs looking for this man and we need to be somewhat subtle. It's not like you and I can just pitch up because we want to see the entertainment.'

'Well, it is a modern day,' said Tiff. 'We could go for that.'

'We could,' said Catriona, 'But if we're going to find out who he really is, what he's doing, we may have to think another way about it.'

8

Chapter 08

Catriona drove through the outskirts of Copenhagen looking around at what she thought were remarkably similar cityscapes to those she would have back home. Of course, there were differences. The language on many of the signs for a start, but here and there were green spaces with trees, other two, three, four-story buildings, many often in red brick. But as she drove into the city, she became truly aware that she had no idea where to find a gentleman's club in Denmark.

'Where would these be, Tiff?' asked Cat. 'I mean, I've no experience. I don't go clubbing and then piling on into gentlemen's clubs—it's not what I do. I'm not sure Luigi would even have been to any.'

'Don't be so sure,' said Tiff. 'I mean, you didn't know he was a thief.'

'He's not a thief. I keep telling you that's why we're doing this. He's not a thief. There's just some confusion over this and we're going to clear it up. I'll tell you what, we'll drive into town until I can see something that looks a little bit seedy and then we'll drop his name, see if we can get some work or something.'

Cat continued to drive further into the centre of Copenhagen and the traffic had started to build. It was the middle of the afternoon and eventually, they decided to park up and begin to look around. There were a number of bars, but much of the area had a classiness to it.

'Side street,' said Tiff. 'They're usually down side streets. I mean, they don't have big entrances generally, do they?'

'I guess you're right. Come on then,' Cat said to Tiff, 'but stay close. I don't trust alleys in any major city.'

Over the next hour, the pair trolled around through the streets of Copenhagen checking down every alley, almost scared to go and ask until they came to a part of town which seemed less salubrious than the rest. The street was clean as the rest of Copenhagen was but the alley was dingy, closed away from the light, and as Cat passed the door she saw an image of a woman posed rather erotically with nothing on.

'We'll try there,' said Cat and marched up to a large black door, rapping it loudly with her fist.

'What is it? We're shut.' Cat banged the door even louder. She heard noises, a man shouting but it was in Danish so she had no idea what was being said. The door opened and a man looked at the pair of them.

'Excuse me,' said Cat, 'I'm looking for some work.'

The man looked down at Cat almost sizing her up and then at Tiff. 'You're English?' he asked.

'No,' said Cat. 'I'm Scottish but I need work. We're stuck here at the university. I can't afford to pay my bills and I need work.'

'What sort of work?' asked the man. 'Do you mean in the bar?'

'Whatever. I have a friend who said that Mr. Clausen took on women for work. Well, I need that sort of work.'

'Mr. Clausen doesn't see anyone,' said the man. Cat looked up at the large black man with wide shoulders dressed in a black shirt and smart trousers. 'Your information is wrong. Mr. Clausen doesn't need to have anyone working for him. Goodbye!' And with that, the door was promptly shut in Cat's face.

'Maybe you just didn't look good enough for them,' said Tiff.

'I'll have you know I can look as well as the best of them.' Cat stuck her nose up to the air and marched off, but it suddenly dawned on her that she had told her niece she looked as good as any stripper in the land. This wasn't really the image she wanted to be giving a younger member of the family. 'It's not helping us though,' said Cat. 'We need to get in. Come on, let's check a few more of these places.'

'He was bothered when you said Clausen. You asked specifically for Clausen,' said Tiff. 'I don't think you should ask for Clausen anymore. Just get a job.'

'But there could be any number of people working these things, owning them. It could take us ages to find Clausen and I don't speak any decent Danish to inquire.'

'Did you say you needed work?' It was a voice from across the street and Cat recognised the English accent. She turned to see a girl of maybe twenty, with long blond hair standing a good six feet two. She was thin and cut more of an elegant figure than most.

'Yes. I need to get work, I can't afford the fees up at the university. Do you know of any work I can get?'

'I do but it's not the best work,' said the girl. 'I'm Emily and I just got out of that sort of work, but I'll tell you where to go if you need it.'

'A friend of mine said Clausen was the man to work for.'

Cat saw Emily's face grimace. 'He pays well; he's not the nicest though. I'm well off out of that. Are you both looking for a job?'

Cat could hear Tiff about to say yes and cut her off with a brutal, 'No. Just me. My sister doesn't need to do that sort of work; I'll be doing it.' Cat wondered what this protective instinct was in her; after all, she wasn't going to do this particular type of work either. All she wanted was to find Clausen.

'If you go around the corner,' said Emily, 'there's a big poster on the wall. It should have a time and a date for some auditions. Mr. Clausen usually likes to vet his own girls so maybe that's where you want to be at.'

'Thank you,' said Cat, 'we'll do that.'

As she went to walk up the street, Emily shouted again. 'Just be careful. As I said, he pays well but he can be a bit hands-on if you understand my meaning?' Cat nodded and began to walk off around the corner. She heard Tiff following behind her, catching up and saying, 'What does she mean he's a bit hands-on?'

That was the thing about Tiff. Sometimes she was so unworldly and that's another reason why Cat didn't want her getting involved in what she was about to do. No doubt, Cat would have to go through some sort of interview process; she might have to dance, jiggle a bit, and she was prepared to do that to clear Luigi's name but not Tiff. Tiff didn't need to parade herself.

The pair stopped in front of a large poster with some ragged edges that clearly had been up there for some days, but from what little she knew, Cat could make out an address and the time.

'Two hours, Tiff; two hours at that address. Get your phone; find out where that is. Then I'll need to spruce myself up.'

'Are you going to start brushing your hair again? It's always the hair,' said Tiff.

'The hair is going to be the least of my worries,' said Cat, 'but I'll need some serious makeup. I need to look a little bit less classy than I do now.'

'Classy? Who said you look classy?' Cat walked off shaking her head; always Tiff there to remind you what you weren't.

Two hours later and after a trip to purchase some makeup, Catriona had heavily done her eyeliner and slapped on enough makeup to make herself feel somewhat tarty. Her mother had always been disgusted when Cat was younger and had put too much makeup on, the amount that forgets anything about how good you looked as yourself. Makeup that didn't enhance but took over.

'Don't you come in with me—stay outside. I'll probably be an hour or two, then I'll come back but I'll have identified this Clausen fella by then. I'll also see what I can do. See if I can break into their offices but I might have to hang about for a bit, so go find yourself somewhere to sit and drink your tea or coffee, or whatever you want to do, but have your phone on you, in case I need you.'

Tiff nodded and quietly walked away, leaving Cat to stand in front of another anonymous door, rapping it loudly. This time a large white man opened it, wearing dark sunglasses. It was almost like a code for a bouncer. Cat advised, in English, that she was here to audition. The man looked her up and down, 'You don't look like someone who would audition for this sort of work.'

'That's because I've got my clothes on, love; once I'm out of them, you'll see I'm perfect for the job.'

The man laughed loudly and waved Cat inside, 'If you come through here, I'll take you through to where you can get changed, Mr. Clausen is coming today, he always picks the girls to work in his clubs. I take it you've worked before?'

'At a number of establishments back home, some rougher than others but you know, you do what you do for the money, don't we all?'

The man laughed, turned around to Cat, 'You do indeed, you'll earn your money here.'

There was a sinister overtone to what he said, and Cat found herself forcing a smile. Maybe there was a bit of fear in her eyes and that may have helped. The one thing that was bringing a smile to her face was the fact that she was acting as if she was a student. Those days were some four or five years ago but they said that she still had it, whatever that was. She can cut a look with the best of them. Of course, this wasn't exactly a high-class establishment, but the look she could cut they would be wanting. Maybe it was more based on that. She knew she would have to be careful.

Cat was shown to some changing rooms where a number of other women were already sitting down, fixing up their hair, applying make-up. A couple of them wore extremely skimpy outfits, and Cat was shown to a rail and told to pick what she wanted off it. As she made her way along the items, Cat realised that there really wasn't going to be a good option. In the end, she lifted off a t-shirt that seemed to be half-cut and some sort of thong. There was a pair of high-heeled boots as well. When she looked at the other girls, Cat thought she was going to get away lightly.

Sitting down in front of a mirror she changed quickly trying not to show any embarrassment in front of the other girls. As she pulled her clothing down, trying to cover as much of herself as possible, she wondered how she was going to get a look around the place. It was then that the large white bouncer came back in and announced that Mr. Clausen was delayed and that the girls would have to hang around for another hour. As the man turned to go away, Cat walked up behind him and tapped him on the shoulder. The man turned around and Cat sidled up to him as close as she dared.

'What's the matter with him?' asked Cat, 'Is this not where he works? Does he not want to pop down?'

'Mr. Clausen is a busy man, and he likes to take his time when he picks his women, so he won't rush. You should get yourselves prepared; you could be here for two or three hours with him.'

'So, he's upstairs working away? Sorting something out before he comes to see us?' said Cat. She suddenly became aware that a hand was running down her back, then made it to her bare cheeks.

'If he is going to be any longer, I'll keep you entertained myself,' laughed the man, 'but he's not here, he's coming in from elsewhere.'

'So, he has lots of other places?'

'He does, I guess you don't realise much speaking only English.'

'No, is this his main place? I guess he has his offices here.'

'Upstairs is where he bases everything,' said the man, 'but

don't you worry. If you make it up there, you'll be doing very well. The girls that go up there don't have to work some nights, if you catch my drift. Now get back in there; he won't be long.' The man smacked Cat's bare bottom. She gave him a little jump and a giggle. 'If he passes on you though, I might give you a night myself.'

Cat smiled but inside she almost retched. There's no way that dirty sod would get his hands on her. It was pretty clear what sort of club this was, or at least what sort of a guy the owner was. She made her way back into the dressing room, then looked around for other exits. There were none but a small man in glasses came through and invited the women to make their way out towards the bar. Then she followed the rest of the girls, and found herself sitting on a high stool, beside the bar and drinking a Martini that was made for her. Cat realised the bouncers just wanted to have a good ogle at all the women, but this would be no good. She'd have to get out and about, around this club, get up to those offices to see if she can find any information up there. *Now*, she thought, *I think it's time to pay a visit to the girls' room.*

9

Chapter 09

Catriona jumped off her stool and made her way over to the bouncer who had smacked her backside a while before, asking where the female restroom was. She then tried to stop herself jiggling as she made her way over to the bathroom. It was around the corner and out of sight and perfect for what Cat wanted. As soon as she was clear of the bouncers, she cut off down a corridor and then away from the main bar area where the girls had been sitting.

The boots she was wearing had rather enormous heels which were loud and certainly could not be run in. So Cat bent down, unzipped the sides, took the boots off, and tucked them away inside a cleaning cupboard she found. Making her way to some stairs she saw at the end of the corridor, she stopped briefly as she heard someone coming down them. Moving into a small alcove, she tucked herself in tight and felt a chill as a door opened and air rushed through into the hole. She imagined she might have to sneak around places, but last time donned all in black with Tiff seemed much more like the sneaking she wanted to do. This time, she was struggling. Tiff would have laughed at how ridiculous she looked, dressed in next to nothing.

Then Cat heard a voice speaking in Danish but only a few feet away. She wasn't sure what to do because the voice was coming closer to her. The man seemed to be shouting back at someone else, but before she had time to do anything, someone stopped right in front of her, scanning her up and down. Cat tried to smile, then realised that the man was wearing a chef's uniform. He blurted out something in Danish, put his hand on Cat's hip and leaned forward. He was clearly angling up for a kiss and Cat decided the best policy was simply to go with it. She leaned forward, matched his lips with hers and gave him a small nip on the backside. The man then broke off, said something to her which Catriona took as something like, 'Later,' and then he marched off.

With hesitation, Cat moved for the stairs and climbed up to the floor above. Walking along the upper hallway, she opened the first door she came to and found a large store containing posters, tickets, and other promotional items. Shutting that door, she continued stepping across the wooden floor, opening another door that had a room housing a small computer suite. Cat wasn't sure where to go next but decided to continue along the hall and came to the last door with a word written across it. She was unsure of what it meant but gently, she began to open the door before it was pushed open and she saw a man standing there. He was dressed like one of the bouncers, and behind him was a bank of TV screens. Clearly, this is where the CCTV footage of the building operated from. She looked around and saw a number of bottles of beer, several of which seemed to have been consumed. On the man's hip was a gun, and he began saying something to her in Danish.

'I don't understand,' said Cat. 'I was looking for the toilets. I only speak English.'

'Back that way and down the stairs,' said the man. 'It's the one with the little lady on it. You English are so stupid.'

'Thank you,' said Cat. 'I'll go to the toilet,' and turned around. As she did so, she felt hands wrapping around her stomach, pulling her back and close.

'I think you need a little lesson for being so stupid though,' said the man. Cat could feel his hand moving up her side and beginning to work in under her top. She struggled but the man's grip was too tight. She wasn't going to take this lying down. Frantically, she glanced around, saw the empty beer bottle, reached with her right hand, grabbed it, and swung it past her head where the man was now nibbling on her neck. The bottle broke on his head and he staggered, releasing his grip on her. Before he could react further, Cat grabbed another of the bottles and smashed it clean across his face. The man stumbled, hit his head on a table on the way down, and lay on the floor.

Cat didn't want to check if he was breathing, and with the amount of cut glass on the floor, she was more worried about where she was standing. Delicately, she stepped out of the office and closed the door. She'd have to move quickly, find out whatever she could, and just get the hell out of there. With the door closed behind her, Cat ran lightly along the corridor, got to the stairs, and went up to the next floor.

There were no higher stairs reaching up beyond this, and then she looked to the left, seeing only two doors. Gently opening the first one, she found a large conference room. Maybe this is where Clausen held his meetings. She didn't know, and looking around, there wasn't much in the room other than a drinks cabinet, table and chairs. At the next door, she found the name 'Clausen' written across it. She opened the door carefully and began to look around the room. There was a large desk in front of her, old-style antique, as well as a number of pictures on the wall. There were numerous provocative women in highly compromising positions, but Cat ignored these and tried to start opening some filing cabinets. Most were locked, but she turned back to the antique desk and pulled out the drawers there.

The first opened easily, and she rifled through papers and pens. She couldn't make much of what was written as it was in Danish or at least some other language other than English. At the next drawer, she found a number of photographs of different women, again, in rather compromising positions. *Was this guy into extortion? Is this what he did?* Because a lot of these women didn't look like girls who would dance at clubs like these. Cat heard a noise and the door began to open. There was no option but to duck down, and she crawled in underneath the desk past a large chair. Someone was there and began walking around. She felt the cold on her buttocks and wrapped her arms across her front. It was one thing to get caught, but to get caught like this, she'd never felt more exposed in her life in so many different ways. There was a slight tear in her eye as nervousness set in. Who knew what they would do to her if they found her like this.

As she waited, listening, Cat saw the inside of the desk and there appeared to be a slight notch in the wood. As nervous as she was, it intrigued her because it didn't look like an imperfection. Rather, something deliberately carved into it. Gently, she reached out with her finger and pushed it.

Some sort of mechanism operated and a spring-loaded drawer popped out beside her head. Cat went to reach up and feel around the drawer, but the legs of a man appeared in front of her and he sat down on the chair. She pulled her own legs back, tucked herself up as tight as she could in the hollow underneath the table. There was a cough and a discussion in Danish, and Cat became aware there were at least two people in the room, but her curiosity was still getting the better of her, and she ran her hand up to the drawer, reaching down into the top of it where she couldn't see. She felt a chain of some sort and gradually pulled it up inside her hand until she felt another item. It was about the size of her thumb and she picked it up, bringing it towards her. Before her, she saw the carving in silver of a panda. On the panda's eyes were set two jewels with a silver necklace tied onto it. It reminded her of the cobra's fang.

Everything about the piece of jewellery that Luigi had given her reminded her of this panda. The style was the same as if they were a set. Maybe that was it. Could this be something that was stolen? Gently, Cat reached up and pushed the drawer back in where she felt the spring lock. Then she took the necklace, tied it around her neck, and dropped the panda inside her top. Maybe she could walk out with it. Once they were clear of the room, she could simply step out, make her way back down, say she'd been to the toilet, and find an exit quickly. Maybe she'd say she'd changed her mind about the interview and had to go. Her mother was waiting, needed care, something like that. Catriona didn't know what, but she needed to get out.

However, she couldn't move until the legs in front of her, of the man sitting on the chair, made their own move. It was five minutes before the man stood up. By now, Catriona's bottom was numb, and then she heard him leave the room. She knelt down closer to the floor to see if anyone else was still there. With no one around the room, Cat crawled out on her knees from underneath the table. She couldn't run away like this. It was ridiculous, the outfit she was wearing. Could she sneak back down and get her clothes again? Catriona stood up and thought about looking further around the room, but she had what she wanted.

She could take this jewel now to the police and say to them, 'Look what Clausen had. Tie him in.' But would that bring her any close to clearing Luigi's name? Still, Clausen was no longer just a name on a botched plan. He was no longer just something on a piece of paper. Catriona pulled her top down, covered herself as best she could, and strode to the door of the office. Before she could open it, the door itself opened and she dived back behind the table, curling herself up as small as she could. She hoped that person would turn and walk away again, but she felt a hand slap her on the backside.

There were words in Danish and then a voice said, 'The English girl, the one that went for the toilet, I see you haven't found it. Up.' Cat didn't move, and then she felt something in her back, something cold and metal. 'I said up.'

Slowly, Catriona got to her feet and turned around to face a large six-foot man with blond hair and a crisp white shirt with black trousers. She hadn't seen him before, but he must've been one of the bouncers. He was holding a gun pointed straight at her face.

'I see you've been busy. I hope you weren't taking something that wasn't yours. Still, there's not many places to hide something, is there?'

Catriona saw the man focus, first around her neck and then looking down to where her cleavage would have been. Was the necklace visible? The man moved the gun forward, put it underneath her top, and started to lift it up gently. Was he able to see the necklace, or was he just some sort of pervert?

'The boss will not be happy with this. How did you find that? No one knows where that is. The boss keeps that to himself.' The man picked up his phone and dialled a number while keeping the gun pointing straight at Catriona's face. He said something in Danish, and then Catriona heard the name Luigi.

'You never should have taken it,' said the man, closing the call. 'How Luigi managed to get hold of it, I don't know but it was the worst decision he made. Was not long before we realised he'd given it to you. Such a pity though,' said the man. He moved the gun back towards the top that Catriona was wearing. Again, he started to lift it up. 'What a waste,' he said. 'The boss said I should dispatch you now and make it clean.' With that, the man pulled the gun back and started to twist a silencer onto the front of it. 'I'm afraid you've got your nose into it too far this time. Still, he chose well. Did the jewel bring you here? Are you that hungry for these things?'

'I came to clear Luigi's name. My husband was no thief.' The man seemed taken aback for a moment. 'You dressed like this for him into here? It's a shame to kill you. A woman with that drive, I'd love to get a hold of.' But with that, he slipped the gun out from underneath Catriona's top and placed it on her forehead. 'Sweet dreams, princess.'

10

Chapter 10

Catriona closed her eyes. This was it. She was off to meet Luigi. One quick pull of the trigger, and that would be her. She waited. Waiting for the moment that no one truly understands. Waiting for, was it searing pain, or was it a quick nothingness like the switching out of the light? Her hand shook. Some people embrace death. Some people can meet it head-on with barely a flap of expression, but not Catriona. Everything began to shake. Something ran through her mind about being found in the state of clothing she was wearing. What would they say? What would the family say?

There was a loud thud which caused Catriona to flick her eyes open. The big silencer that had been placed on her head had fallen away. She looked down at the bouncer lying on the floor unconscious. Now standing in front of her was Tiff in a bikini, holding a very heavy marble statuette. The top half of it had seemingly cracked, requiring her to have two hands on it to keep it from falling to the floor.

'Thank God, Tiff. I thought I was gone.'

'I knew you couldn't handle it. I knew you'd do something stupid like this and get caught, and all for nothing, probably, too. We need to move. Apparently, there's a commotion. They've been trying to call somebody, and he isn't answering.'

'I think the boss is on his way,' said Catriona. 'That guy was talking to him on the phone before you clubbed him.'

'Let's go then,' said Tiff. 'I hear footsteps coming up the stairs.'

'Heck, no. Come on, Tiff, we need to find some other way out. Shut that door.' Tiff closed the office door, and together, the girls moved a filing cabinet across to block the entrance. It was heavy, but they were up against it.

There was banging on the door. Then Cat heard a gunshot, and then another one, the bullet of which entered the office and hit the back wall. Tiff was over at the window. She threw it open and stepped outside onto a small metal platform beside which was a fire escape. Catriona threw herself out and followed Tiff down the metal steps.

'What about your gear?' said Tiff.

'Forget it. There's nothing important in there. I didn't take any cards or any identification in there, I'm not stupid. It's all back in the car.'

'The car is halfway across town,' said Tiff.

'Exactly. We need to go somewhere else.'

As the pair reached the bottom of the flights of stairs, they heard a door opening up further down the alley. A man stepped out with a raised gun. Cat turned and began to leg it out into the street. A number of cars braked suddenly as the pair, dressed in their skimpy outfits, made their way across the road. Cat saw some rather interesting looks from many of the drivers.

'We've got to get off the street,' said Cat. 'We can't run around like this.' Casting a glance over her shoulder, she saw several of the men coming out from the club, stopping traffic and crossing the road behind them. Cat didn't look as she got onto the pavement of the road, and bumped into a man wearing a large black coat. He gave her a serious look, and his hands reached for her before Tiff collided into him as well, knocking him onto his bottom.

'Sorry,' shouted Cat, as the pair ran off along the street. 'We need to get out of here.'

'It's blooming cold, too,' said Tiff. 'Can you see anyone with a coat?'

'Never mind a coat, somewhere inside; we need to go inside.' Cat grabbed the door of a nearby shop, running inside. The shop was full of clothing, but a watchful assistant was keeping an evil eye on the pair as they entered.

'We can't stop. We've got to keep going. Those guys are only just behind us. We need to lose them first.' Cat ran on through the shop with her hand held behind, pulling Tiff too. She rounded a corner of clothes, smacked into a gentleman who was calmly standing beside his wife. He caught Cat up in his arms, and she instantly stared up into his face.

'Sorry,' she said. 'Thank you,' and give him a quick peck on the cheek before running off. She barely heard the slap on the man's face as his wife advised him that that sort of behaviour was not appropriate when out with her.

Cutting out through the rear door of the shop, the pair entered the shopping centre and ran up an escalator. Cat's feet were sore, and they were cut by the metal grooves, but she didn't stop at the top of the escalator. They ran around the balcony area with more shops before descending down into a car park at the rear. From there, they exited out into the sunshine of the street, albeit, with the cold wind whipping around them.

'Have we lost them yet?' asked Tiff.

'I don't know,' said Cat. 'We keep going. Look.' Across the road, Cat could see a leisure centre and made straight for it. Entering at the front, she ran past the reception. Hearing splashing and smelling the chlorine, she cut off to the swimming pool.

'Enter the showers, the lady's showers,' said Cat. The pair sprinted inside a cubicle, pressing the button. Water fell down on them, Tiffany indignant as her trainers had started to become soaked.

'Where do we go from here,' asked Tiff.

'It's the women's showers. They can't just walk in, can they?'

'But we need to get some clothes and get back out. Did you see any lying around?'

'I'm not sure. They're all in lockers.'

'You just want us to half-inch some clothes?' said Tiff.

'Yes, needs must, and look,' said Cat, pulling up her top. Despite the inappropriateness, Tiff realised Cat was showing her the jewel hung around her neck. She reached forward looking at it closely.

'That's just like your cobra's fang, isn't it?' asked Tiff.

'Exactly, Clausen had it. The fang is not just a one-off. Maybe that's why it was stolen; maybe it's got something to do with that.'

'Okay, but you need to get out and find some clothes, Tiff.'

'Why me?'

'Because I'm in a thong and a top, and am now soaked through. You're in a bikini; you look like you should be in a swimming pool. I look like I belong in a top-shelf magazine at the moment.'

'Don't flatter yourself,' said Tiff, exiting the shower. Catriona stayed under the hot water, her hand shaking from the chase. Yes, they were free now, but they could have been followed in here. Embracing the hot water of the shower, Cat could hear a bit of commotion. It appeared that someone was popping their head in to the shower units, somebody was searching. The men can't come in, there would be screams. Instead, it sounded more like disgruntlement. Cat wondered what to do and then she pulled off her top, took off her thong, held it close into her chest, keeping her back to the door of the shower.

She heard the door open next to her shower unit and a woman complain. It was only a few seconds later when her own opened. Cat let out a shriek in Italian and began to chatter away in Luigi's native language about the disgrace of what was going on. She thought there was an apology, maybe in Danish and whoever it was moved on.

Cat continued to shower and listened as more doors were opened before the changing room seemed to settle down. Shortly after, the shower door opened and she heard Tiff's voice, 'You can come out and get changed. I've got some stuff. People leave anything lying around; did you know that?'

Cat placed her clothing down and reached into the bags Tiff had brought. She managed to find a pair of jeans and a T-shirt but the underwear was never going to fit. As it was, most of the rest of the clothing was snug, but all they had to do was get into the car. Once they were in the car, they would leave Copenhagen, pick up some clothes elsewhere. Cat looked across at Tiff, who had also changed out of her bikini, but unlike Cat, the clothes Tiff was wearing seemed to fit remarkably.

'You lucky sod, how did you get such a good-fitting pair?'

'I picked them. There was a number of items so I checked through each of them before bringing them.'

'You didn't check for my size, though, did you?'

'I'm not sure that the Danes are your sort of shape.'

'What exactly is that meant to mean?'

'Well, bigger than me.'

'The term is curvaceous,' said Cat. 'Come on, get changed—let's go.' Catriona threw the wet clothes she changed out of, along with Tiff's bikini into the bags they had removed the external clothing from, then she watched Tiff place them back exactly where they had found them before. Cat fumbled inside frantically and found a hair tie, tying her hair straight back and tucking it inside the top she was now wearing. She advised Tiff to do the same. That was the thing. It was all about looking different. Then she saw a baseball cap, sitting in a bag to her left. Grabbing it, she placed it on her head and advised Tiff to follow her.

As they exited the changing rooms back into the reception of the leisure centre, Tiff could see a man in a black jacket sitting in the cafe, staring into the swimming pool. She immediately put her hand out, stopping Tiff for venturing further forward.

'That guy over there,' said Cat. 'We bumped into him in the street, we put him onto his backside. Do you recognise him?'

'I don't recognise anybody. We were running around like anything. How can you recognise him?'

'It's him. Look at that eye, one of those eyes isn't looking, I think it's glass, the one on the left. Whatever it is, we can't go near him. I think he's been looking out for us. This way, come on.'

With that, Cat tried to make for the front door, but then she saw a man standing in a white shirt, black trousers with his back to her. His shoulders look like a sideboard and all she could think of was he was a bouncer. She turned with Tiff and began to read some posters on the wall.

The man was conversing in Danish and he seemed annoyed and angry, but shortly he stopped talking and left the building. Cat decided to wait for a while. After more study of the posters in the wall, the two women eventually made their way through the front door and began looking around.

They could see to one side a number of large men walking around the pavement looking about. Clearly, they were still a prime target. Cat saw an older man coming over to the leisure centre and immediately went up to him and linked an arm around him. She reached up and gave him a kiss on the cheek.

'Tiff, take his other arm.' Her niece seemed reluctant, but at Cat's urging, she eventually did. The man was surprised, but he did not stop their attention. Together, the three of them walked out to the street, the two women looking up at the man all the time, and not looking around. When they reached the street, the man turned, continued to walk along and after about two minutes, Cat began to stop him.

'Thank you, sir.' she said, reached out and kissed him again on the cheek. He had a bemused face, but he was smiling and said something in Danish. 'Time to go, Tiff.' said Cat and strolled off along the street. 'Do you know where we parked the car?'

'No. I don't have my phone with me either. I left it where I hid all my stuff. It's quite a few streets away from the club where you were having your interview,' said Tiff. 'We'll circle around and pick it up. Once we do that, I might work out where the car is.'

'Good.' said Cat, 'I think we get the car, we drive out of here, we find another town, we buy some clothes, and we get out of Denmark. The next nearest address is Bruges. Time to head for Belgium, Tiff. I think Denmark has just become too hot for both of us.'

Meanwhile, in the leisure centre changing rooms, a distraught woman was looking at the wet top and thong that was now sitting in her bag and wondering how on earth she was ever going to get home.

Chapter 11

Catriona drove their hire car down to Falster, a small town south of Copenhagen, where they picked up some new clothing before they began to settle in for the drive out of Denmark and into Germany. From Germany, they would cut across, route from Bremen, then touch into Holland before arriving down to the picturesque town of Bruges in Belgium. It would take a couple of days, and as soon as they were well clear of Denmark, Cat pulled into a hotel where she slept for eight hours solid. Tiff as ever, did not seem to require much sleep, at least not in the normal times of the day and Cat was woken up to find her drumming on the wall.

'I think it's a collection,' said Tiff. 'There might be a number of things for us to find, definitely a collection.'

'I did actually think of that myself.' Cat reached down inside her pyjama top, pulling up the panda jewel and looking at it. It reminded her so much of the cobra's fang, but it also sent something distasteful running through her. Had Luigi stolen all of these? Would he be involved? Surely not. She knew her Luigi. Yes, he was rash, he could be excitable, but he was no thief. Luigi stood on the right side of the law.

'We could, of course, just hand these all in. What we've got so far,' said Tiff.

'And do what with it? They think Luigi was involved, stole these items. If I hand in another one it just says he did, especially when I hand in plans that says how he stole it. There's only names like Weiss on it. We need to go through and find these addresses, find out what really happened. We need to bring a complete story. We won't be able to clear Luigi's name unless we do that, and that's the point, Tiff. This is not an excitable jaunt; this is about clearing Luigi's name.'

'I know that,' said Tiff, 'but just be aware, we may not be able to do it. Even if we get everything returned back to the bank it came from, it's going to be hard to prove Luigi wasn't involved.' The girls tidied up the room, pulled what small bags they had together, and got back into their hire car. Cat was sticking mainly to smaller country roads and she preferred to drive at night, but they set off before sundown and were now routing briefly on an autobahn. After three hours, Cat began to feel weary at the wheel, tired from looking in the rear-view mirror where she thought she saw the same car over and over again.

'Tiff, the same car's behind us. It's been behind us for a while now.'

'We're on the autobahn, of course we're going to have a car behind us. It's like that, isn't it? You travel the same way, you go roughly the same speed. It could be anything, slow down and we'll see.'

Cat reduced her speed and the blue car she was watching passed her. Tiff looked across. 'That's a family. It's a family with kids,' said Tiff. 'You're just getting paranoid; we're out of Denmark; we shook them. They're not with us anymore. Just calm down and we'll get onto where we're going next.'

'Maybe I'm just excitable,' said Cat. 'I am tired of all the running around and now driving as well. Maybe I should pop in for a coffee, take a break for half an hour before I drive again.'

'That sounds good,' said Tiff. 'I can get some sweets.'

Tiff's ability to always look for sweets in times of crisis astounded Cat. Everything went back to what Tiff needed, never what Cat needed. There was no concern of, 'Yes, you need the caffeine. Let's go and find what you want.' It was always what Tiff wanted. Still, she was with her. Not many people would have gone this far. If it had not been for Tiff, Cat might have been dead by now and it would have been something for her to don a bikini and come into an establishment like that. Maybe she didn't fully understand it—who knew.

At the roadside services, Catriona pulled up and the pair made their way inside. Tiff insisted on buying sweets first before they headed to the small self-service restaurant. It wasn't always easy to be healthy at times like these. Cat managed to fill a large plate, her hunger overcoming her nervousness. Tiff ate next to nothing but then that was normal for Tiff; then she'd soon stuff up on sweets.

As they got up from the restaurant, Cat looked through the large glass windows into the car park where she could see her car sitting under a floodlight. Most of the car park was well lit and she could see a man standing close to her car. He had a large leather jacket on and she thought she recognised the face from the leisure centre.

'Tiff, look, that man over there, look at him. What's he doing? That's that bloke. He was the one that was looking at us, the one we bumped into on the road.' Tiff stood and stared out the window. 'Don't watch him like that, he'll see you.'

'No, he won't,' said Tiff, 'these are reflective windows. You can't see in, you can only see out, but you're right, I think that is the guy from the leisure centre. How are we going to get him away?'

'I don't know but we need to get him away from the car.'

'I think it's time we sat down again. We can always get up if he moves. While we're in here and he's out there, he hasn't seen us. It looks like he's clocked the car though.'

Two hours later, Catriona was sitting at the table still looking out at her car with the man sitting in front of it. Surely, he would move soon, or maybe he was scared to in case the women came back.

'Tiff, he hasn't moved. What can we do to move him?'

'Wait it out,' said Tiff. 'He'll have to go at some point, and I've got a plan but we need to wait; otherwise, the plan won't work. So just drink your coffee because you'll need to be awake to drive.'

'Awake to drive? I'm going to need a commode, the amount of I've coffee I've drunk.' Catriona yawned and stretched her arms before she saw Tiff suddenly leap to her feet.

'He's on the move,' she said, 'come on, follow me.' Together the two women made their way to the entrance and Catriona followed Tiff as she made her way up behind parked cars, keeping the man in sight.

'Down low. Stay low.'

'This looks a bit suspicious though, doesn't it?'

'I don't care if it's suspicious, we need to keep low—he can't see us.'

'Where do you think he's going?' asked Cat.

'Back to his own car, he needs something. Look at him, look at the way he keeps turning around and watching our car. He needs something from it, probably a snack or something. He doesn't want to be too far away in case we come back.' Tiff was right; the man was watching their car. Cat saw him open his boot and take out a small bag from which he removed some sandwiches, stuffed them in his mouth, and then took out a flask. Cat watched him carefully drink, all the time studying the car he had left. When he was done, he placed the items back into his boot, closed it, and walked backed over to Cat and Tiff's car.

'Well, that's us back at square one,' said Cat.

'No, it isn't. This is perfect, but we need to go inside and get some fruit.'

'Fruit?'

'We need fruit, lots of it, lots of fruit. Something reasonably squashy though, not too big, not too wide.'

'I don't follow, Tiff, I really don't follow.'

'You don't have to follow; just do as I say. Keep low as we get back in.'

Together the women re-entered the services. Tiff made her way over to a small supermarket where she grabbed several bunches of bananas before telling Cat to pay for them. 'Okay, this is the fun bit,' said Tiff, 'You need to walk out, let him see you, and then let him chase you.'

'What are you going to do?'

'I'm going to make sure we can get away but please do it subtly and bring him inside here, lose him somewhere in the services, then run out to the car, jump in and go. I'll be out here waiting for you. I'll maybe need about five minutes though.'

'Are you sure about this? This seems an awfully big risk. We might be better trying to find a bus or something, or somebody that'd give us a lift out of here.'

'Trust me,' said Tiff. 'Just trust me.'

Catriona made her way to the front entrance and watched as Tiff stepped to one side, still holding a large bag of bananas. Slowly Cat walked up towards her own car, not lifting her head. Then when she was maybe thirty meters away, she looked up, made sure the man knew she was making eye contact with him, and then turned and ran back inside the services. Once inside, she made for the stairs that led to an upper level, turning round on him to see the man in the black coat following her. He was quick.

Cat walked at pace around the balcony at the top of the services. The man was keen not to be seen to be rushing after her, but she also felt he was gaining. She cut into a shop and hid down behind a large amount of lingerie. Men always seem to be embarrassed in that section; maybe this guy would too.

Crouching down, Cat stared out from behind a rack of bras and could see the man staring at the door of the shop. The assistant walked up to him and asked him something, possibly if he needed help. The man shook his head and continued on into the shop. He walked slowly through, searching thoroughly. Cat could feel her hands beginning to shake again.

The man at the club had put a gun in her face. Who knew who this guy was—did he work for them? She hadn't seen him at the club. What did he know? It was as the man grew closer that Cat realised that she had backed herself into a corner. Behind her were some changing rooms, but this rack was out on its own. As the man came towards it, Cat tried to keep herself bent down. He had seen her go in, he had searched every other part of the store, so surely, he must know where she was. She was either behind this rack or she was in the changing rooms.

Cat thought some part of her must be sticking out from behind the rack, because the man approached, and in German asked if she would be so good as to look for his wife in the changing room. Clearly, he was trying to get Cat to pop out, to show herself, so he could identify her. She was trapped. Would she be quick enough to go either side of the rack and make a run for it?

Cat bent down and looked at the base of the rack holding the bras. It looked fairly unstable, and reaching down, she grabbed the two metal bars that led out to the feet that the entire stand was resting on. Quickly she pulled them up, and thew them as hard as she could, causing the entire thing to topple onto the man on the other side. It wouldn't hold him for long, but she didn't need long. Tiff had said five minutes. Hopefully, she'd had that.

Cat bolted from the shop, knocking several other stands over in the process. There was a shout from a security guard, but Cat wasn't listening and ran for the stairs, taking them two at a time. Behind her, she saw the man emerge from the shop, but she kept running out to her car. In the strong lighting of the car park, she could see a different figure standing beside their hire car. Pressing the button, the doors opened, and she saw that person get into the passenger side and Cat jumped into the front seat.

'Nice one,' said Tiff. 'Now let's get going.'

Catriona started the car and in the rear-view mirror, she saw the man emerge from the services. He took one look and ran over towards his own car. As Cat began to drive, the other car began to move, then stuttered and came to a stop, jerking all the time.

'Go,' said Tiff, 'Just go.' He's not following us anywhere.' Catriona put her foot to the floor, pulled out onto the autobahn, and just kept driving. She kept looking in the rear-view mirror but now everything was just lights.

'Are you sure he's not behind us, Tiff? He could be behind us. I wouldn't know; I can't see anything.'

'He's not behind us. I told you I'd take care of it. Just drive, we've got a long way to go. If we drive through the night, we won't be that far off Belgium. I think I'll get some shut-eye.'

'No, you won't; you keep an eye on the road and make sure he's not following us.'

'How is he going to follow us? Remember that bunch of bananas; he's got all those bananas stuffed up his exhaust. That car is not going anywhere.' Catriona turned and stared at her niece and then she began to laugh. Sometimes Tiff just surprised you and this was one of them.

$$12$$

Chapter 12

Catriona and Tiff entered Bruges on what was a cool but sunny day. The compactness of the town with its central square that seemed to be a pulling point for all tourists, gave an indication of the impressive architecture that was everywhere in the small town. Every time Catriona looked up, she saw something else jutting out from a building, some delicate piece of masonry, small faces or unique curves that could bring tears to any art lover's eye.

Among the chocolate shops, small museums, and shops, Catriona and Tiff were looking for a small museum of beer. Cat was well aware that beer in Belgium was different to the somewhat crass lager that was often drunk in Scotland. Although Scotland had its own diverse range of darks and malts, the Belgian wheat beers, especially those brewed by several monasteries, had developed such a reputation that despite the strength of the beer, people still sought it in reasonable quantity.

But it wasn't the beer that the women were looking for.

Mertens was the name associated with the address. Mertens, that was written on the bank-robbery plans. *Why a small museum of beer?* thought Catriona as she struggled to park the car in the busy town.

Together the pair walked the streets, often over cobbles, and brushed past tourists on every side. Luigi had once brought her here and they'd sat on a veranda as he ate his steak. Bleu, as they said, very pink inside. Catriona had preferred hers better cooked, but she'd enjoyed the mussels that came in large buckets served up to your table in a white wine sauce. Memories flooded her head of their time spent here walking the streets and picking up delicate chocolates and dropping them in her mouth.

And the charming hotel had memories that would redden her face. Bruges had been a good place for them, a good place to be away from everyone, but now it was something secret, something different. Luigi knew this place. Cat had known that because when they came here, he required no map in a maze of streets. Had he been part of a scene? What was so special about this small museum of beer?

It took half an hour to locate the building, but once spotted, Tiff and Cat bought a pair of tickets to walk around the small exhibition. It was set on three floors, and you had to make your way to the top before descending through each floor. On the second floor, the museum detailed how the crops were grown that would later be part of the beer. The fermentation process was displayed and smaller working diagrams of previous breweries, some incredibly basic and old, were laid out for tourists to walk around.

Tiff stared at each individual item, scanning it. She was sure that they were now looking for a collection of similar jewels.

Cat thought Tiff was fighting herself not to ask Cat to show the panda jewel hanging around her neck. At times Cat wanted to take it out, compare it with the little friezes and displays that were on show, to see if she could spot something within them that was similar in fashion, but she resisted and instead acted as if she was just another tourist enjoying her time abroad.

As they made their way to the first floor, Cat glanced at Tiff, and she gave a shake of her head. Neither of them had seen anything of note on the second floor and now here on the first floor, they were to learn about bottling plants and labels and the history of how the beer was advertised. Cat walked among friezes which had little models of men standing with the great machines. Another display showed a man capping bottles by hand in an old-fashioned method. It was funny because bottled beer seemed so ancient, and yet it had not been that long ago it was the only beer—long before draught was invented.

Standing looking at a frieze showing an advert on the wall for a brand of beer she did not recognise, something caught Cat's eye. At the back of the frieze, apparently standing in a field, was a tall crane with its feathers tucked in tight, its neck bent over slightly, the long legs impressive. What really caught Cat's eye was the jewel sitting in the bird's body. It was red, possibly a ruby. One thing was for sure, it was the same overall style and design as the panda jewel. Cat waved Tiff over.

'Tiff, have a look at this. It's good.' Tiff half-shook her head, looking at one other frieze before Cat insisted that she came over. Tiff looked at the poster on the wall of the frieze, scanned around it, and shook her head at Cat who pointed a finger into the background of the frieze in response.

'That's it, isn't it?' said Tiff, becoming excited.

'It is. Don't lose it. Nice and calm. It's inside this box, and

I can't get in to get it. I don't know how we're going to steal this.'

'We're not going to do it now,' said Tiff. 'There're people watching us. We should move on a little. We'll come back around and look at it again.'

The girls continued to wander around the exhibition and made their way back along the same level and instead of descending the stairs, simply returned back into the room where the exhibition was. This time, Cat tried to get in and behind the box to see what was behind it. There were a number of wires and she thought it looked alarmed, although she couldn't be sure it wasn't some of the electronics running into the frieze.

But somebody put it there deliberately. If so, why not just simply lock it up? Or had they put it in plain sight? After all, it was an unusual jewel, not something you'd see all the time. Maybe some people might think it to be cheap tat, a little plastic ornament stuck in the back of this frieze.

The next time they left the exhibition hall, the pair descended the stairs to the ground level to go round the last part of the museum. Here there were samples of beer, but Tiff and Cat's minds were on something much higher above when they spilled out onto the street. Cat led them to a nearby cafe, where she sat down for some black coffee and ordered a number of chocolates to come along as well. Well, they were in the right place for that and they would look like tourists.

'How are we going to get it?' asked Tiff. 'I mean, we can't just do it there and then. It's a bit obvious if you break into the back. Did it look like it was alarmed?'

'It's just a load of wires going in, but the thing has lights and that. I can't tell, can I? What do I know about electrics?'

'Maybe I should have had a look,' said Tiff.

'Tiff, what do you know about electrics either? Nothing. Let's face it, neither of us do. It's going to have to be a smash and grab.'

'But it's on the first floor,' said Tiff. 'If we grab it and somebody sees us, they can close it all off. We've got to get down those steps and out of the way. You can't just leap out of the window, you'd break your legs.'

'Then we need a diversion. Some other reason to get out.' Catriona sipped her coffee and plonked a chocolate into her mouth.

'Well, you come up with something, then. I thought my aunt was cleverer than this.'

'I'm eating a chocolate. It helps me think. Quiet.'

'I suppose I could distract the guard. Or maybe you could do that. You always say you're the better one at talking to people.'

'I am the better one at talking to people, but you don't have the sleight of hand to be able to get that thing out. You'll have to break into the box. It'll have to be a concerted effort. Do you think it was free-standing on the plinth it was on? If we knocked it over, would it smash?'

'Possibly,' said Tiff, 'but we can't knock it over because they'll look at it afterwards, won't they?'

'Unless we're in a hurry. A hurry to go somewhere, a hurry—'

'To get out,' said Tiff, almost shouting.

'Shush, don't draw attention. But you're right, to get out. If everybody were trying to get out, it could get knocked over, we could grab it, you could fall on it, grab something from it. Then we'd have the perfect excuse to leg it. Why would we want to get out?'

'Fire,' said Tiff; 'we'd need to start a fire.'

'That's a bit extreme,' said Cat. 'I mean, what are you going to do? Just charge in waving a blazing timber about?'

'We don't need a full fire, we just need something that gets everybody out of the building,' said Tiff. 'Maybe I can put a lighter up to one of the fire systems. It doesn't matter if it's a false alarm. We all get out, then they all come back in again. The key thing is they don't know, so they all hurry out anyway.'

'One other thing,' said Cat. 'When? Do we do it later in the day?'

'We could do it as soon as I get a lighter. It wouldn't be a problem. Well, what's the problem now?'

'I keep thinking people are watching us. I haven't seen anyone in a black jacket, but I just keep getting the feeling we're being observed.'

'You're probably just a little hyper after all that's happened, but don't worry. I've got my eyes on the situation,' said Tiff. 'If we're being followed, I'll know about it.'

Catriona did not feel as confident as Tiff that her powers of observation would be up to this, but what choice did they have? They needed this jewel to help clear Luigi's name.

'Let's make a move and do it,' said Tiff.

'Well, let's make sure we're prepped up first. We get everything ready with the hire car, park it somewhere we can get out of Bruges quick if we have to. We don't want to be hanging on anywhere.'

'It's a good idea,' said Tiff. 'We'll go, we'll pack up, we come back. We come back with very little. You should really leave that panda jewel in the car just in case something happens to us. We don't want to give up what we've already got.'

'That's smart thinking, Tiff, because if they want that as well and we don't have it, it's going to be a lot more likely they keep us alive.'

'You think they're not going to keep us alive? These people just want their jewels.'

'Tiff, I had a gun put to my head. Somebody is not messing about here. You and I have to be careful we don't get caught up in something big. It's why I didn't want you to come. The very least I want is you going back in one piece to my brother.'

'But I'm having such fun,' said Tiff.

'All the same, we need to keep an eye. Let's go pack the car, get what we need, come back, and get this done. I don't think we'll stop in Bruges, as much as I'd love to.' Cat looked down at her coffee and picked up another chocolate. Dropping it into her mouth, she remembered Luigi having chocolate to drink at breakfast and thinking it was ridiculous. That was, until she joined him. Of course, breakfast was up on a balcony looking out over the town. She remembered the crisp white robes that were shed once they were back inside the room.

Yes, Bruges held some great memories for her, but now there was a little distaste in her mouth. Had this been a stomping ground of Luigi's? Had he hidden this crane jewel in the beer museum? Who was Mertens, anyway? Regardless, it was time to go and get sorted. Cat took the cup to her mouth to drink the last coffee before throwing another chocolate into her mouth. 'Time to go, Tiff. Let's get sorted.'

The women made their way back to the car and then drove it to the outskirts of the town. Having deposited all of their clothes into the boot except for what they were wearing, Cat took off the panda jewel and hid it inside the car. They'd get in, they'd get out, no complications. As they journeyed back into town, Cat kept glancing around her, looking over her shoulder.

'Stop that,' said Tiff. 'People will think someone's after you.'

'Someone is after us. We have to be careful,' said Cat. They walked down in one of the narrow streets leading to the centre of the town and the large square where a large stage had been erected. There was a vibrant beat coming from the band that were on the platform and the pair found themselves having to push through the crowds to make it back out to the small beer museum. By the time they'd purchased their tickets again, there was only twenty-five minutes' opening time left.

'The timing's good,' said Tiff. 'Not that many people in here either. We should be able to get out and then disappear off. I doubt they'll open again if we've all just been kicked out for a fire alarm. Probably a good chance to go home early.'

'I'm not sure the Belgians think the way you do,' said Cat, 'but let's hope so. Anyway, up to the top level, then I'll make my way down. You need to give me three minutes and I'll be in position. What's your watch say?' Cat noted the time. 'Okay. I'll let you know when I'm ready.'

The girls climbed the stairs to the top level and Cat found it hard to start reading anything in the museum, having passed through it before. All she wanted was to get this jewel in her hands, which were now shaking, so she stuffed them into her pocket. Halfway along the upper floor, she turned to Tiff.

'Three minutes from now. Go.' And then walked off. Cat made her way down and onto the middle floor, casually looking around, but glancing at her watch several times. Two minutes left. She needed to slow her pace. Standing in front of a large board, she pretended to read it, but she could feel her feet beginning to tap and drove them onto the floor, determined that they wouldn't give away her nervousness.

She shuffled along, gradually coming closer to the exhibit she wanted to be beside. There was a small party up ahead looking at the frieze this time. Cat wished they would move off. Thirty seconds left and they were still there. She moved up behind them, peering, trying to squeeze in. It was no good. One of their children was pointing into the frieze. The father at the child's shoulder was laughing too. Ten seconds. She'd have to get into position now.

Catriona was never a rude woman, although when she was determined, some people might take necessity for rudeness. So it was, as she elbowed the group's mother out of the way, almost fell on top of the father and knocked the kid sideways. The father went to speak and an alarm bell began to ring. Cat spun round, knocked into the frieze on purpose and it tumbled to the floor, smashing. Cat pretended to fall over, looked across and saw lying on the floor, a long metallic crane with a red ruby inside.

13

Chapter 13

Catriona reached over and picked up the gleaming jewel, holding it tight in her hand. Around her, people were starting to move visibly towards the lower floor as the fire alarm continued to ring. Picking herself up, Cat quickly smoothed down her trousers before walking in a brisk, but steady fashion behind others towards the stairs, down to the front exit. Around her, two museum curators began telling everyone to stay calm and to move in a reasonable pace in various languages. Cat recognised Italian, English, and of course, French and Dutch.

As she reached the stairs, she was pushed behind by someone and fell into the gentleman from the family she had barged in front of when trying to get at the frieze. He turned and stared at her, grimacing and muttered something in a language Catriona did not understand. Ignoring him, she continued down the stairs and out of the front door into the street beyond. Across from her, Tiff was smiling, but also giving a questioning face, hoping that everything had worked out. Cat raised her arm up and held in her hand the jewel, so that Tiff could see it.

Afterwards, Cat would remember an elbow clipping her shoulder, someone coming past her at pace and ripping the jewel from her hand. At the time, she simply spun around and fell to the floor, scraping her left knee hard on the pavement.

'Cat!' shouted Tiff and Cat looked up to see her niece running towards her. There was a look of horror and shock on her face. After taking a moment to stare at Cat, Tiff began to run off along the street. Catriona pulled herself upright, shook off the arm of a concerned man, and began to quickly gather her thoughts. The jewel was no longer in her hand, it was gone. Someone had hit her, then taken the jewel. Tiff must've seen it. Cat looked up, saw Tiff turning a corner up ahead, and began to run after her. Catriona sprinted hard, puffing as she went, regretting not being in better shape.

However, Tiff was in good shape. Maybe she could keep up. Catriona was fortunate enough to catch a view of Tiff's head as it went left, and then right, and then left again. Then she turned the corner. Cat was suddenly in the large market, the centre of Bruges, a large flat area where often the market was held beneath the view of the Belfry of Bruges. The entire area was like a small amphitheatre with roads running around the outside and the towering Belfry looking down from above. Cat imagined someone being up there, giving a thumbs up or a thumbs down to some great gladiatorial fight in the past.

Of course, this was ridiculous. Now the only fight was past other people searching for trinkets and food at the market stalls. At this time, there was a large stage set up beneath the Belfry and a band was playing. People were mingling with a beer in hand, dancing, laughing. All of this made it almost impossible to see Tiff. Cat ran, pushing people aside, desperately trying to find her niece.

'Tiff, Tiff, where are you? Where are you, Tiff?' There was no cry back above the noise and hubbub of the crowd and Catriona continue to push forward. Then, off to her left, she saw the crowd break as a small scuffle was breaking out. As Catriona got closer, she saw a man with a woman on his back. The woman was small, thin, and had long brown hair. As the man spun around, Cat saw the determined face of Tiff clawing at the man's chin. He reached up, placed a hand on her shoulder, and as he then rotated at the hips, he threw her forward over the top of himself, hard onto the cobblestones.

The crowd gasped and some man leaned forward to try to stop the perpetrator of the act from escaping, but he threw a punch as Catriona broke through the crowd to reach down for Tiff. The would-be policeman was knocked to the floor and the man began to run.

Cat grabbed Tiff under the shoulder, hauling her to her feet. Her niece looked stunned, but Cat took her hand and began to run after the man who'd only recently thrown Tiff from his shoulder.

'Keep going, Tiff, keep going. We need to keep going.' Catriona felt like she was dragging a tonne weight. Tiff's legs kept going and somehow, she remained balanced as they raced down the pavement, shoving happy tourists out of the way. There were cries of, 'Watch it,' and other things in foreign languages, but Cat really didn't care. The jewel was ahead, the man slowly disappearing from sight. After a few hundred meters, they came to a bridge over one of the many canals that run around Bruges. The road itself split left and right or crossed over into another overhanging street, but Cat could not see the man on the road and desperately spun around looking for him.

'Tiff. Come on, where is he? I need your eyes. Look around. Where is he?'

'I don't know. My head, it's sore.'

'I don't care. We need to find him. There, he's on that cruise barge. It's just departing. Look!' Catriona watched one of the river barges packed with people start to peel away from the quay side. The canal was below the road, some six or seven feet down, and the barge was moving slowly with the man at the rear of it. He was clearly trying to look like a tourist, attempting to blend in, but Cat recognised the jacket. The man was also sweating, breathing heavily.

Turning around, Cat looked at Tiff. She plunked herself on the floor. 'It's spinning,' said Tiff. 'It's all spinning around. I can't—I can't—'

Cat spun back and the boat was still on the move. She ran off the bridge to the road that went tagged alongside the canal. The boat was moving out into the centre of the canal and beginning to pick up a little pace and Cat was not sure if she could keep up by running alongside with it. Soon it would disappear. The road would break away from the canal and Cat would lose the man. Where he would get off, who would know. Looking back quickly at Tiff, she decided her niece was not going to be of any use at this time and quickly pulled off her top, leaving herself in a T-shirt and trousers. She kicked off her shoes, ran, jumped onto the wall that ran beside the canal, and got herself up to alongside the riverboat as it moved out.

Catriona may not have been the most athletic person, but the one thing she could do was swim and swim well. Her arms were strong, her legs could kick. Luigi had always told her she had almost a fish-like quality within the water. Cat was never quite sure what that meant. Did she look sleek, or was she scaly? Sometimes Luigi had said things and she never caught the full drift of them.

She took one step, pushed off with her foot, and dived out into the water. Making an entry was second nature to her. As she went under the surface, she let her motion carry her back to the top and began to crawl forward with her arms. Her legs kicked hard, and she could see the boat was only a couple of metres away.

Amidst her splashing, Cat could hear the cries of the people on the riverboat and the occasional glance saw it rock from side to side. There was obvious confusion and the boat seemed to slow down, allowing Cat to catch up on it and put her hand on the edge. A pair of arms came down, pulling her up and onto the boat. She saw the smiling face of a young blond gentleman. The person she really wanted was at the rear of the boat. Helpful hands hindered her as she tried to make her way along the boat, people asking was she all right when all she wanted, was the jewel from the absconder in the rear.

Looking at the man now, she could see he was her own height, wiry and thin. That didn't mean he couldn't pack a punch. Catriona was not a fighter but something inside her was burning. Her beloved Luigi's name was at stake, and someone was trying to stop them. She had already had a gun held to her head and this man was not going to get away. He was going to hand over the jewel. The boat was going to go to the side of the quay and Cat was going to get off, shake herself down, find Tiff and move on. That was what she envisioned. However, the man seemed to have other ideas. Now standing at the back of the boat, he found the pilot telling him to sit down.

The man stepped forward, his compact frame approaching

Cat. She reached for him, seeking to find the jewel he had. He managed to grab her and put her into a headlock. Cat was unsure what happened next. Somebody must have hit the man because he fell down releasing Cat's head. She turned around and saw the blond twenty-year-old who had pulled her from the water, smiling and the man with the jewel already picking himself up. He made a jump into the water and began to swim back towards the quay side. Cat doesn't hesitate, taking two steps and launching herself into the water after him. She was clearly a stronger swimmer and found herself gaining, so much so that she was able to grab the man's ankle as he started to pull himself up onto the quay.

She kicked, pulling backwards with everything she had. She was unable to protect herself when he took his other leg and planted a foot firmly onto her forehead. Cat fell backwards, deeper into the water and tried to relax, allowing herself to float back up. When she broke the surface, she saw the man running along the quay, heading back towards the bridge. Quickly, she swam, pulling herself up, water dripping from her as she began her pursuit.

The man was turning onto the bridge but then he fell, hard. Because of the sides of the bridge, she couldn't see what had happened. That didn't stop her running, taking the steps two at a time, getting back up onto the street, where a number of tourists were standing around looking shocked at the scene in front of them. Tiff was lying on the floor, and the man was beyond her picking himself up with a bloody mouth.

Catriona padded forward, her wet clothes making a slopping sound, but as she got close, the man began to run again. Catriona saw Tiffany put out a hand and she grabbed it, pulling her niece up to her feet.

'You're soaking.'

'So was he. Follow those wet footprints. Come on, we need to go. He's still got the jewel.'

After swimming exertions, Catriona was struggling to maintain any pace. Stamina was not her strong point and despite Tiff now having some sort of semblance of balance, she too was not in full flight. Watching the wet footprints, Catriona followed them, first right, then down a small alley, in through the back of some houses, and then out into another street.

The man was out of sight. He had left a trail, one which Cat intended to follow but she understood that without increasing their pace, they would never catch him.

Across the street, she saw a pair of bikes sitting against a shop with no lock on them. The shop was a patisserie, a cake shop. Inside she saw a young couple purchasing and realised they must have been their bikes. *Oh well*, thought Cat. *I need to take those. Hey, they've probably got insurance.*

With that, she dragged Tiff over, picked up a bike, and jumped on it, cursing as she felt her bare feet struggling against the pedals. There was a cry from the shop as they pedalled off, but Cat didn't look back to see the owners of the bikes. Instead, she followed the wet footprints round the long street and down another ally. After that, she found herself in another road, the houses piling up on either side. There was something about the streets of Bruges, where they overhung like some comic medieval fortress. Regardless, she pedalled on, Tiff in her wake, until she realised she was coming to the edges of Bruges where the river circled it.

At the end of the road, she could see a multiple junction, but on the far side of it was a large brick structure with an archway running through it. In the archway, she saw the man, still sodden and breathing heavily but holding out his hand. In front of him was a woman, blonde, voluminous hair, but in smart jeans and a leather jacket.

As Cat got closer, she saw the woman take something from the man's hand. Surely it was the jewel. There was a quick glance up from the woman and she spotted Cat hurtling towards her on the bike. The woman turned, ran across the road, and right onto a small footpath that led between trees, along the riverside. Behind her Tiff was shouting, pointing at the man but Cat shook her head.

'Through the trees, Tiff, the blonde woman. We need to get the blonde woman.'

14

Chapter 14

The path cut through the trees, running alongside the main river around Bruges. There was a light wind, the trees blowing back and forward, and the sun had just broken through the clouds causing the shadows to dance. The blonde-haired woman was running at an impressive pace, but Catriona and Tiff were on bikes, and they were soon catching up on her.

Cat thought the easiest thing would be to ride up, jump off the bike on top of the woman, and bring her down, but as she got within five metres, the woman reached into her pocket, turned round, and pointed something at her. Cat's mind instantly said gun. She threw the bike to the side, tumbling off and onto the grass. She could hear the laughs of the woman and then heard Tiff crash into the bike behind her tumbling over the top of her. Cat pulled herself back up to her feet racing over to her niece who was laying on her back, breathing heavily. 'Come on!' cried Cat. 'We need to keep going.'

'But the woman's got a gun,' said Tiff.

'The police will be after us too. She's got it. She's got that jewel and we need it. I need it to clear Luigi's name.'

'We'll be dead before you do that.'

Catriona stared at her niece urging her on but in her own mind there was a calculation racing. Would she be dead? Would her efforts to stand by her former husband mean she'd end up joining him in the afterlife? Was it really all worth this? He had been her love. He had been the only one in this life who had really been able to lift her up, who really understood her, and they wouldn't call him what they had called him. He was no thief. She was sure of it.

'Tiff. Come on!'

Although Catriona was running as hard as she could, the woman was clearly much more of an athlete and despite the fact she was not dressed for sport, the blonde-haired woman kept a keen pace. It wasn't long before Tiff overtook Cat. Her lighter and nimbler figure able to maintain a quicker pace as they continued the route alongside the river of Bruges, before crossing over a bridge. It was made of brick with several arches beneath their feet allowing the water to pass through. The iron railings on either side gave the essence of a quiet, calm place but there was nothing quiet about Catriona's breathing as she made her way across. Part of her felt like the sick was going to come up from inside but she drove herself, continuing on to another path that led through more trees.

The blonde-haired woman turned a sharp left at the end of the trees closely followed by Tiff and as Catriona managed to reach the end of the tree-lined avenue, she saw a sign pointing towards a train station. Was that it? Was that the idea? Was this how the woman was going to leave?

The station carpark was busy with buses driving here and

there. Catriona saw numerous people heading out from the station, the train obviously having just arrived, but she didn't have time to look, time to see the various pizza outlets and other food kiosks. Instead, she made for the main hall looking for her niece and the woman who had the jewel. Unlike the tree-lined avenue, there were numerous blonde heads moving about, here and there, amongst a sea of other people, and Catriona struggled to find out where was the target she was looking for.

Cat approached some barriers and saw Tiff arguing with a conductor. The representative of the train company was insisting she couldn't go through, that she had no ticket. Cat turned and ran towards an automated machine pressing whatever button came to mind. She pulled her sodden purse from her jeans, took out a card, passed it into the machine hoping it would read and then breathed a sigh of relief when two tickets jumped out of the bottom.

'Tiff, it's okay, we've got some.' She ran up to her niece, pulling her away from the conductor. Cat saw the man's face looking at this woman, sweating and sodden through as well. He gave a little shake of his head. Being from an older generation, maybe he just thought she was a student on a prank, but whatever, he allowed them to pass and they made their way onto the platforms.

The station had a number of platforms all parallel to each other, and accessible by heading down to subways that ran underneath the tracks. Standing on the edge of the platform, Catriona looked around for the blonde-haired woman, anxious to know what train she would be getting on. She looked up at the station's electronic signs to see which trains were due. Platform three was here in two minutes and Catriona looked over, picked out the number and then scanned that platform. There was nobody, but then again, maybe she was waiting down below so she can run up, jump on the train and get away quickly without them knowing she had departed.

'The subway Tiff, platform three. That's where the next one goes from. Come on.'

'But why? Why would she be going to platform three? Who's going to Ghent?'

'I don't know if that's where she's going but that's the next one to leave so if we're on that platform she can't go. Come on.'

Catriona raced down the steps, her feet hurting on the solid floor beneath them. She wasn't used to running barefoot but so far, she'd blocked out the occasional stone that had appeared underfoot. Now her feet were cold, and she was sodden, beginning to shiver and starting to feel down. Had they lost her? Had they come all this way and blown it? Running up the subway steps, Cat emerged out onto platform three and told Tiff to go to one end while she went to the other. There were several people waiting, all giving Cat rather bemused stares but she ignored them seeking out the blonde-haired woman. When Cat found no one, she met Tiff again back at the subway steps in the middle of the platform.

'She's not here,' said Tiff. 'She's got to be somewhere else. Another train.' Catriona spun around, searching from platform to platform. On platform six she saw a blonde-haired woman with her back to her. Could that be her? She was wearing the same coloured jeans. The top looked similar too. Tiff tapped her on the shoulder. 'Platform two, far end sitting down on the ground. I think she's trying to cover something up.'

'There's someone out there on six,' said Cat and thought to

herself, *we need to cover off both sides; otherwise, they could lose her*. 'Right, Tiff, you go to two, see if it's her. If it is, shout, I'll come back. I'll go to six, if it's her, I'll shout too.'

With that Catriona turned and ran down the steps. In the subway, she pushed her way back, causing murmurs from people calmly going about their everyday business. As she approached the subway steps, Catriona hurdled them, taking as many as she could and then regretting it when she got to the top and was struggling for breath. She walked out onto the platform. She stared along and saw the jeans she had seen before and the voluminous blonde hair. The woman turned and looked at her, gave her a slight smile and put her hand in her pocket. In the distance Cat could see a train coming towards her.

'Tiff, it's six. Tiff, it's six.'

'Coming,' said Tiff, loudly. Catriona saw the woman shake her head. Again, she tapped her pocket indicating the gun that must be in there and pointed to the nearby train. Catriona walked closer, slowly, carefully, and watched the woman's hand slide inside her jean pocket and something caused an indentation that pointed towards Cat.

'I give you this. You're determined but I think this belongs to me. Don't come any closer. I will shoot.'

'In this crowd?' said Cat. 'I doubt it.'

'It's got a silencer on it. They won't hear. They won't realise until this train is gone. Don't come any closer.' Catriona stopped in her tracks and stared at the woman. She was slightly taller than Cat, maybe by a couple of inches and certainly looked leaner and fitter. *Bet she can't swim as well though,* thought Cat. Her mind was racing. How was she going to get this jewel? The woman had a gun.

'It's safely inside my bag,' she said. 'And it's coming with me. Don't make me do this. I want to see you again. I know you're not stupid enough to have the other jewels on you, but you have collected them so we will see you again and we'll come to get them too. Mr. Clausen is very annoyed although I think it was rather careless of him.'

Catriona watched as the train pulled up and the doors opened. A small number of people began to get in but only the blonde-haired woman stepped between the double doors in front of Cat. Cat followed her closely.

'No, no. You're not coming on board. You stay there.' Cat could hear the beep, the doors would be closing soon and the woman would be gone.

'You'll be needing this,' said Catriona pulling down her top and showing the panda necklace around her neck. The doors began to close but the woman stuck her foot out causing the doors to beep and open again.

'Give it to me. Throw it in now. I don't have to shoot you.'

'You won't shoot me anyway. You'll be seen taking the jewel off a body. It'd be easier if I came in there.'

'No. You stay where you are unless you want a bullet in the head,' said the woman, taking the gun out from her pocket. 'You'll undo that necklace and you'll throw it in here to me.' Again, the doors beeped, began to close but her foot stuck out making them open again. Catriona could see a guard beginning to move down the station platform.

'Now,' said the woman, 'undo the necklace.' Cat reached behind, slowly undoing it, shaking as she saw the gun pointing towards her. Putting the necklace in her right hand, she looked at the panda realising she was now giving up everything. She didn't have the fang either. Who was this woman? The trail will be going cold and Cat's exploits will have been in vain as she'll have none of the jewels.

'Throw it,' said the woman.' Cat moved her hand backwards, about to throw the jewel through the door but then she saw a shadow behind the woman. Something hit the woman hard in the head causing the gun to drop, and Cat saw Tiff ripping the bag from the woman's arm and stepping out of the train as the doors began to beep. The woman tried to stumble forward but Tiff pushed her back in. The doors closed and the train began to pull away.

The conductor came up to Cat announcing something in French which Cat thought meant, 'Is there a problem?'

'Drunk person, sorry,' said Catriona. 'She pushed me in the water earlier. We're going home now.'

'You should do; you're all warm—hot and bothered. You could do with a shower. Freshen up,' said the conductor. 'Can I help you?'

Tiff put her arm around Catriona.

'It's fine. I'll see her home.' Together the women walked briskly back to the subway, stepping down until they were out of the light. Only then did Tiff open the bag. There were a number of items, but sitting at the bottom of the bag was a Korean jewel with a red Ruby behind it.

'We got it, Tiff. We've got it. That's two.'

'We need to get out of here. Look at the state of you. Time to go,' said Tiff.

Catriona nodded. 'Time to go, but we need to get to Luxemburg and do it quick. Somebody else is on this. She said Clausen was annoyed. I don't know if she worked for him or she works for somebody else. Tiff, we need to be quick because I don't know who else wants these jewels.'

15

Chapter 15

The TV in the service station showed pictures of Bruges, of people reporting a chase. It was reported as nothing but a minor commotion, including a woman who had dived into the river and swam about in pursuit of a man. The host on the TV wondered if there was a romantic attachment between them, questioning whether or not the relationship had gone sour. Cat nearly choked on her soup when she found herself being described as an irate woman with no sense of decency. At least the whole incident was put down to some lovers' tiff. Clearly, the museum hadn't noticed the disappearance of the crane jewel which now swung around Cat's neck along with the panda.

'Luxemburg next. Did you see where the address is?' Cat asked Tiff who was deep in thought looking at her phone.

'It's in the woods just outside Luxembourg City. It looks like it's away from everyone. Jones was the name attached to this. It doesn't sound very European, does it?'

'It does not,' said Cat. 'But you can't tell, can you? If there was a crew brought together to steal from the bank, they could have come from anywhere, and who knows where they've settled? When you steal things, I guess you have to make your bed wherever you can find it. Some countries might not want you back.'

'Are you still feeling cold?'

'Well, thanks, Tiff. You don't normally ask, but no, I'm okay now. I think the heat in the car has sorted me out. Change of clothes helped as well but my hair is still messed up.'

'Here,' said Tiff. 'I went and got you this from the services.' She handed over a small packet wrapped in brown paper and Cat opened it gently. Inside was a hairbrush. It was cheap and plastic, but it would do the job. Almost immediately Catriona began to brush through her hair. There was nothing like being properly groomed.

'I usually wear a swim cap going into the water. It seems to help a bit, especially with the chlorine and that. Who knows what was in that river?'

'I'm fine, too,' said Tiff. 'I did get a bash on the head.'

'Well, you seem yourself.'

'Well, I was quiet on the way here.'

'That's what I mean,' said Cat. 'You seem yourself. Distant, looking off out of the car. Didn't seem that much was wrong to me.' She saw Tiff roll her eyes.

'Come on. Let's get going. If we keep going through the night again, we might arrive at a reasonable time tomorrow, be able to search for the house in the daylight.'

'I think it's best that we don't check into any hotels or places,' said Cat. 'With these people also looking for these jewels, we want to give as little clue as possible to what's going on.'

'Agreed,' said Tiff. 'I don't mind sleeping in the car anyway. I can sleep anywhere.'

Lucky you, thought Catriona. *My hip will play up; my leg will go to sleep in the wrong place. I'm not looking forward to it, but best get on with it.*

Travelling through the night was taking its toll on Cat and with the exertions of the day, she found herself having to pull over three times and give herself a slap right in the face to stay awake. *Tiff didn't notice*, thought Cat. *Flat out asleep, but maybe she could take a watch when we arrive so I can get a nap in the back of the car.*

Across the border into Luxembourg, Cat barely saw the difference between the fields of Belgium and the open lands with clumps of wood stuck between the arable crop growing vast squares. It was along one of these roads into the woods that they found the house they were looking for.

Stopping the car about half a mile away, Cat told Tiff to sit in the front while Cat took a nap in the back. Tiff agreed and soon Catriona was curled up on the seat, her mind racing, but her eyes closed and sleep fast arrived. When her eyes suddenly flicked open, she wondered what was wrong.

'Tiff? Tiff?' There was no reply. Cat sat up suddenly and realised no one was in the front. *Oh heck*, she thought. *She's gone to scope the place by herself.* Stepping out of the backseat, Cat locked the vehicle and made her way along the roadside until she could nip inside the woods traversing across a thick forest. She used her phone GPS to make sure she arrived at the house.

As she got close, she saw it was a simple, small bungalow, possibly three or four rooms with an ornate garden around it. On the side of the house was a large window looking out across some fields—the only view of the house that didn't look into the thick forest.

Who knew why those trees had been chopped down? Why was there was no arable land out there? It must have given a pleasing sight to those inside. As she looked more closely towards the window, she saw a figure crouching down and realised it was Tiff. Shaking her head, Catriona made her way along the side of the forest before sprinting across in a half crouch and joining Tiff.

'You're meant to be sleeping. I'm just getting the lay of the land.'

'What are you doing going off on your own? What happens if you get caught?'

'Don't you talk to me. I'm the one who's pulled you out of it. You've had a gun stuck in your face twice and I sorted you out.'

'This is crazy,' said Cat. 'Don't go off on your own. Promise me.'

'All right. Stop sleeping through the daytime.'

I drove all night, thought Catriona. *Doesn't she get that? She slept. I drove in the dark, eyes straining. Sometimes you can't win with Tiff.*

A door opened at the rear of the house. Both girls suddenly crouched in tighter to the wall. Someone was outside and they heard them start to make conversation. Tiff looked at Cat who realised that the man was speaking French. It was difficult to hear but it sounded like he was ordering some sort of woman. A masseur by the sound of it. She would be out at the house that night at five o'clock.

After a short and brisk conversation, the call was hung up and the girls heard the man retreat inside the house. They kept their place for another hour, but still there was nobody visiting the house and the man did not come outside. Mozart was being played. Maybe he was relaxing, who knew? It was a strange place, so far away from everyone else, hidden out in the wood, but then it was discreet. Maybe the man didn't want to be found.

The women made their way back to the car and drove off to find somewhere that served food. Sitting in a café together, they contemplated what action to take. Clearly, the house needed searching, but the man was inside and he sounded like he could be there for the night.

'What about this woman who's coming at five? If we intercepted her and you went in as her, I could go inside secretly,' said Tiff. 'I'm quite good at searching and finding things.'

'That might work,' said Cat. 'After all, it's only a masseur. I think I can manage that. Was able to rub my hands correctly for Luigi but we have to be smart about stopping her.'

'His drive is quite long. He won't see her if we can intercept her on the first part. We'll just tie her up, put her off to one side. Let her go afterward.'

'It all sounds a bit risky,' said Cat, 'but it's the only plan we've got. Otherwise, it means going in and if we surprise him, he'll come at us. This is a good idea, a better distraction. See if you can find what you want and get out before anything happens. I don't think we can waste too much time.'

'But nobody's after us. We lost them back there. I mean, they don't even know what car we're in.'

'No but they knew where the museum was,' said Cat. 'I bet they know where everyone is. Maybe they're watching us right now.'

Tiff looked around her. 'No. This place is clean. I checked it when I arrived.'

Catriona shook her head. Tiff had an amazing belief in what she could do and while at times, she was very impressive, she clearly was not a master spy able to spot anyone on her tail. Not that Catriona could do any better. It was half-past four when the women parked the car up half a mile away. They made their way along the main road and then hid at the side of the driveway. When a white car pulled in, just after five o'clock, Catriona stepped out blocking its path. The woman rolled down her window and Cat advised in French that she was from the police and was worried about people in the area. She apologised but said she would need to check the woman's car.

When the woman stepped out, she covered her mouth with her hand, kicked the back of her knees, and watched as the woman dropped down. Tiff came along and tied up the woman's hands and together they took her off to the bushes, hiding her there. As they placed the woman in the undergrowth, Cat caught Tiff's eye and watched the smile on her face. So far it was all going well.

Catriona went back to the car and drove up to the house, knocking on the door. She had taken a bag from the car with her and when she heard the door opening, she smiled broadly, tilting her head so her hair moved back of her face.

A bald-headed man, possibly in his sixties answered the door. He was tall, about six foot four but looked quite out of shape. The man stepped to one side allowing Cat to come inside. She then jumped into the air as she felt a nip on her bottom. She turned around, giving the man a stare but he smiled cheekily and pointed her on into his main lounge. There in the middle of the floor was a large towel and the man told her in French to get ready while he would get himself undressed. Cat stepped off to one side, undid the bag and realised that there was a skimpy set of scrubs within it. She also noticed a set of handcuffs. Fluffy handcuffs. Maybe the woman was more than a masseur. She was beginning to wonder had she heard correctly?

When she turned around, the man was lying face down, stark naked on the towel in the middle of the room. Quickly she donned the scrubs, realising too late that they were rather tight and revealing. The man looked up and smiled and Cat told him she'd just left something in the car. With that, she nipped into the hall, opened the door, and saw Tiff's face as she ran inside.

'They're a bit over top,' whispered Tiff.

'Just hurry up,' said Cat. 'I'm not going to be like this for long.'

On returning, Cat saw the man smiling and he asked her to start on his shoulders and work down. Cat made her way to the bag, took out some oils, and poured them on the man's back. Gently, she began to work his shoulders and work his arms. He was patient, just lying there but Cat could tell he was excited. As she worked on his back, the man started asking would she not be more comfortable wearing a little less. Cat said she was fine as she was but maybe they would look at that later, but for now she wanted to work on his back. As she reached his hips, the man raised himself slightly, jiggling his buttocks and telling her he felt a pain in and around them.

Come on, Tiff. Come on! Cat placed her hands on the man's backside, kneading it gently, and heard him cry out to do it harder. She quickly pressed hard then moved to his legs but by the time she got to his feet, Cat could see he was getting quite excited.

'Time for the other side,' said the man in French and spun

himself over. Cat was a woman of the world but the sight before her was not a pleasant one. She told the man to lie there and she'd be just a moment. Disappearing into the bag, Cat wondered how long she could string this out for. *Where was Tiff? How much had she searched? Had she found anything?* Cat was all prepared to make sacrifices, but this was about to get too far. She went to turn around and realised the man had stood up and was now inches from her.

He reached out to her shoulders, telling her she'd be freer with nothing on but Cat pushed him and began to run away.

There was a laugh from the man, and he began to follow her, round and round his living room furniture like some sort of comic seventies movie. Cat was finding nothing funny. When the man chased her into the kitchen, she decided she'd had enough. Looking around, she saw a set of kitchen knives and pulled out what she thought was the largest one. Spinning on her heel, she pointed the knife at the man advising him in French to stay back. The man clearly thought this was part of the act and made a motion that Cat thought was quite lewd.

He lunged at her again and Cat ran off, opening the door. They only succeeded in moving across the hall into the bedroom. On her knees in the corner, rifling through one of the drawers was Tiff. The man ran in excitedly but then stood in horror, realising there was another woman in the room.

'What's he getting so worked up about?' asked Tiff as the man began to shout in French.

'He's wanting to know what's going on. He says he didn't pay for two, he says one is enough. Besides, he doesn't like stick insects.'

'Who is he calling a stick insect? That's ridiculous.'

'He says he prefers somebody more curvaceous.' What frightened Cat was the way she actually enjoyed that comment. 'He says he's going to call the company; says he's going to get them to sort it out.' Cat stepped forward, knife still in hand. She told him not to bother and that maybe he should lie down and she would sort it. Maybe they both would sort it.

The man grinned. Clearly thinking his luck was in, he laid down on the bed. Once he was there, Cat made sure that the knife was hanging close to a part of him he would not wish to lose. She pulled out her top and the man hungrily looked up until he suddenly saw two jewels hanging on necklaces fall from Cat's neck.

'Where is yours?' she asked in French. 'Where do you keep yours?' The man shook his head saying he didn't know; he didn't understand what she was asking. Cat moved the blade closer to the man's skin. 'Tell me now,' she said, 'or you'll lose it.' The man's face was now white and his hand reached over pointing towards a picture on the wall.

'On the side of that, Tiff; look on the other side.'

Tiff spun the picture around, and there in the back was a necklace, and hanging at the bottom of it was a silver Tiger with a blue jewel behind it.

16

Chapter 16

'It's time to go,' said Tiff. 'We've got it.'

'You speak English,' said the man. 'Who are you?'

'I don't think you're the one to be asking the questions,' said Cat, still holding the knife close to the man's own family jewels.

'Don't,' he said. 'Don't, but don't take that. No one should know about that jewel. It's not for anyone else.'

'Why? What do you mean, no one should know about it? Where did you get it from?'

'The bank. We stole it. Surely you know that.'

'We need to go,' said Tiff. 'We can't hang around like this.'

'Get the handcuffs. There were handcuffs in the woman's bag,' said Cat. 'We'll handcuff him to the bed. That way, we can get away quicker.' Tiff nodded and exited the room, and Cat turned her attention back to the man.

'You stole them with Luigi, didn't you?'

'Who's Luigi?'

'Don't. Don't try that. Luigi was very dear to me even though he's gone, so I want to know. Tell me you stole it with Luigi. Why did you steal it? Why did he want it?'

The man's face was total amusement. When Cat pressed the knife closer, he became deeply agitated.

'I know nothing. I don't know this man. Who are you talking about? There was five of us. He was not one of them. Maybe he used a false name with you. I don't know.' Tiff entered the bedroom, saw the man's face, and looked at the position of the knife and almost began to laugh. She took the man's hand and handcuffed it to the bed.

'You can drop the knife act now. Go on, you better go and get changed. We'll get out of here quick,' said Tiff. 'I'll keep an eye on him until you're ready.' Catriona nodded, but she wasn't happy with the man's answers. Making her way to the other room, she began to dress, putting back on her jeans and her top. Taking the bag she brought in, she collected Tiff, and together, the girls made their way back to the white car parked outside.

'That was all too easy,' said Tiff. 'There's only one other place left to go now, Weiss and Liechtenstein. Are you going to drive through the night again? Are you okay to do it?'

'Did you see what he was looking for?' asked Cat.

'I saw where you were holding the knife. He wasn't that sort of a guy, was he? Looking for those sorts of thrills. I mean, one slip of the knife and—'

'No, he was not. He was looking for the more straightforward kind of thing.'

'And would you have, to get the jewel?'

Catriona shook her head, looked out the window and then turned to her niece, 'No, I'm a lot of things, but I'm not that.'

'No. I didn't think you were,' said Tiff. Catriona felt a

glimmer of pride in her niece, delighted that she had at least some sort of higher opinion of her aunt.

'Should we untie the woman?'

'No, it won't be long. She'll get out of that,' said Cat. 'Best we just put distance between us and here. She's going to have a hard job explaining why she's there, tied up. It's all the better. But he obviously didn't want to lose the tiger jewel, did he? There were also signs that he wanted to keep it quiet. I don't think we'll get that many problems from him.'

'But you can't tell, can you? I read about these things.'

'You read too much,' said Cat. 'We go get the last one, we get to the bank, and hand this stuff over. That way, we can clear Luigi's name.'

'I still don't see how you're going to do that,' said Tiff. 'All it says is, you knew where everything was, like a robber would.'

Cat cast a glance at Tiff with her eyes that said, *don't go there.* The car trundled down the road and Cat swung it round to the right. The road went quite steep before turning back on itself yet again. The vehicle was clearly going too quickly, and Cat pressed down on the brake in what should have been a routine manoeuvre around the corner. She felt the pedal go flat, no resistance, and the car was out of control.

It ran off the side of the road and began to pick up speed as it went down a small hill. There were trees around it, and it soon smacked hard into the base of a large oak. The emergency bags exploded, and Cat felt her face being driven into hers before she was pulled back into her seat. Her mind was groggy, her head was spinning, but her first instinct was to look to her right and see if Tiff was okay.

The girl looked shaken, but she was breathing. As Cat went to put her hand up on her shoulder, she heard a tap at the door.

Turning back, she saw a gun looking at her through the glass. Then the door opened, and the owner of the gun looked inside.

'Out. Out now!' came a cross voice. He was speaking English, but clearly was no native.

'I'm coming. I'm coming,' said Cat and turned slowly to be picked up by the shoulder and flung out of the car onto the ground. She was soon joined by Tiff, who arrived abruptly, rolling to a halt.

Catriona looked up at the man who was taller than her and strong. He was wearing a white T-shirt that clung to his body, his muscles clearly on show, and a tight haircut revealed an imposing neckline and chin.

'I don't want to hurt you, but I will,' said the man. 'You've been searching for a number of jewels, and I believe you have them. They don't belong to you, and I don't know why you have them, but you will give them to me.'

'I'll do nothing of the sort,' said Cat. 'Who do you think you are here?'

'He's got a gun,' said Tiff, quietly but deliberately.

'I know he's got a gun,' said Cat, 'but you don't threaten people like this. Besides, he's bluffing.'

'I won't bluff. If I have to, I'll kill you and pick them off your dead body.'

'If indeed I have them on me,' said Cat. 'You don't think I'd be so stupid enough to carry them on me.'

The man seemed to contemplate this before stepping forward, grabbing Tiff's hair, hauling her up and pulling her round in front of Cat. The gun was placed at her head. Cat saw Tiff start to cry.

'Give me them now, or I'll blow her head off,' said the man.

Catriona went to speak, but she found her mouth dry. She

realised it was her niece this time at the end of the gun, not herself. Surely, the man wouldn't do it, but had she got that wrong?

'Now,' said the man, and Cat saw his trigger finger begin to move.

'Here,' she said, 'here.' She pulled down the front of her top, taking off the necklaces, collecting all three jewels.

'That's better,' said the man. 'She shall be pleased, and she'll be here shortly. Give them here.' Cat took her three necklaces, crawled forward, and placed them at the man's feet. As she did so, he threw Tiff towards Cat. Her niece fell over, rolling again hard on the ground, and Cat made her way over to wrap Tiff up in her arms. Tiff's tears hadn't stopped, and the girl was having some sort of breakdown, shaking.

'I'll come for you for this?' said Cat. 'My husband was Luigi, and us Italians, we don't take this sort of thing lightly.'

'You don't sound very Italian to me,' said the man.

'I tell you; I am the wife of Luigi. You may have been partners with him once but not anymore.'

'Who is Luigi?' asked the man, clearly confused.

'Don't try that on me,' said Catriona. 'We know about the plan. We know about the bank, whatever's been taken. You did it with Luigi. Now, you want all of it for yourself.'

'Look, lady,' said the man, 'I don't know who you are. All I know is what you're carrying. My client wants it. I will give it to her. I send her that, she pays me the money, and I forget everything, so don't try and plead with me. I am not someone who's going to do anything about it. Cat got up on her knees, but the man stepped forward and kicked her, knocking her back to the ground. 'Just shut it. Don't speak till she gets here.'

Catriona held on to her niece for the next five minutes until a black car pulled up and a woman got out of the rear. She nodded to the man, who turned and handed her the jewels. Each one was picked up and inspected, slowly and carefully.

'You've done well,' said the woman before turning to Cat. 'Where is the fang? Where is the cobra's fang?'

'You took the cobra's fang,' said Cat. 'You were the one with it. You were the one who stole it.'

The woman sneered, moved her hand behind the back of her head and untied her hair. Cat recognised the voluminous blonde and watched the eyes that had previously put a gun on her face. 'Why are you following us?' asked Cat.

'Because you have the items.'

'Do you know where to go?'

'I know where the last one is but I'll get it, so don't trouble yourself. In fact, let me put you out of trouble. Once I'm clear,' said the woman to the hitman, 'I want you to get rid of them. You can have some fun with them if you want, otherwise, quick and clean. Put them back in the house. Anyone else in there, kill them too. That'll be a good mystery for the police to look at.'

The man nodded, and Cat saw the woman make her way towards her black car.

'Why did you do it? Why did you do this to Luigi?'

'Who's Luigi?' asked the woman. 'Who exactly are you?'

'He's going to kill me. The least you can do is not lie to me. You stole it with Luigi. Be upfront and honest with me. You stole it.'

The blonde-haired woman turned around, shook her head, 'I don't know who Luigi is. You're crazy, sister. You're crazy, but I thank you. You've made my job a whole lot easier. It's a pity you couldn't finish it.' As the woman turned away, Cat spat at her, but the man stepped in, slapping Cat with the back of his hand.

'Not until I'm away. Five minutes.

Catriona slumped to the ground turning to see Tiff still writhing, crying on the floor. 'You don't have to do this to us,' said Cat.

'But I do,' said the man. 'It's in my contract. It's why I get paid. Shut up.'

Catriona bent over and began to cry. *This will be it. Killed on the side of the road in Luxemburg. This is to be my fate for trying to clear my husband's name. Damn you, Luigi, she thought. What did you get into? What's this you brought onto me?* Inside, an eternal clock was ticking the minutes. Surely, two had gone by now, maybe three. Catriona looked up, saw the hitman starting to step from side to side on his feet. He was keen to get going, obviously, keen to tidy up this mess. It was then that she heard something. Looking up to the roadside, she saw a group of nuns walking along, their white habits bobbing from side to side. The man looked at Cat, and she saw the nervousness in his eyes.

'Help us,' cried Cat. 'We're destitute. We need shelter. We need shelter, sisters.' She repeated the cry in French, and the man stepped towards her, quickly glanced back and then stuffed his gun inside his pocket.

'They're women,' said one of the nuns and began to rush down the side of the hill, sliding to a halt beside Cat. 'How can we help?'

'We need shelter,' said Cat. 'This kind man, he found us, but he can't take care of us. We need good women to look after us. Those who can spend the time.'

More of the nuns had now made their way down. 'We're

out walking,' said the woman in French. 'Maybe that's why He made us go this way. God is good, is he not?' She turned to the gunman. He still had his hand in his pocket. 'Thank you, my child. You may go. You've done a good deed today bringing these two to us. Go.'

Cat watched the man's face, clearly deciding if it was worth killing a group of nuns as well as Cat and her sister. When he simply walked away, her heart skipped a beat.

'You will come with us,' said the sister. 'Come with us, and we'll feed you and clothe you. God is good, is he not?'

'Oh, yes,' said Cat. 'God's bloody good.'

17

Chapter 17

The jewels were gone. Catriona stood outside the nunnery, awaiting a taxi, in a desperate urge to get to the final address that was on the robbery plans. The nuns had saved them, taking them away from the man who would have killed them. There was the mess that was the car to think of as well, but that could all be sorted later. Right now, Catriona needed to get to Lichtenstein, specifically Gaston in Lichtenstein, the home of Weiss, whoever he was, or maybe it was a she. They might be too late, of course. It seemed that the woman who had ordered their killing was on her way somewhere already.

The nuns had been a little bit amused when Catriona picked up her phone and dialled for a taxi, but she explained that they were not destitute, merely that the man who was holding them had trapped them.

'Should she call the police?' the nuns had asked.

'No,' said Cat. She just wanted to get away, and these decent Christian women had let her do what she wanted. There was a practical side of Catriona taking over, working at what to do next, but of course, the game was almost up. She did not possess any of the jewels. She had no way of proving Luigi's innocence. The other side of it was that nobody seemed to know who Luigi was. Maybe he had used a false name when working with them, if indeed he had been working with them. How had darling Luigi got involved in any of this? Cat was bemused and frustrated.

Tiff had gone silent on arriving at the nunnery. Maybe it was the fact that everything had gone south. Maybe it was the fact that it looked like they were going to lose. Tiff was never good at that. Tiff had to win, had to know she could do something, but the truth was that in life, you lost more than you ever won. Catriona knew that, and she won the biggest prize of her life. And she had lost him shortly afterwards.

The gear, of course, was still in the car that had crashed, and Catriona wanted to get back there to remove it all before phoning into the hire car company and advising of the accident. She would come back and deal with all that, pay for the car if necessary. She had the funds. Maybe next time, she would simply buy a car, but this time, she'd go pick up her gear, get into town, get a new hire car, and head for Lichtenstein.

Europe was a funny place. Everyone thought that each place was unique, had its own special flavour and character, but in truth, Catriona found that they all started to blend into each other, especially at the speed they were travelling through it. When she had stopped at the resorts which Luigi travelled about, quite often she woke up without knowing what country she was in, and in a lot of them, the language did not change. The accents varied here and there, but that was true even of the UK, and it meant she could manage to negotiate any country.

There were very few that stuck out differently.

The taxi arrived and Catriona called for Tiff who was sitting on the step of the nunnery. A young nun was sitting with her and as Tiff stood up, the nun blessed herself, then blessed Tiff before waving goodbye.

'Who was that?' asked Catriona as Tiff arrived at the taxi.

'Who was who?'

'The nun, the one that was blessing you.'

'What nun?'

Catriona was truly astounded at times at how much Tiff could live inside herself and not see the very things outside her. Either she just wished not to acknowledge them, or maybe she thought there were difficult questions coming. Either way, Catriona did not care and ushered her niece into the taxi. The driver looked a little astonished when they asked him to stop beside the wreckage of another car and Catriona disappeared down the slope, cleaning the interior of their belongings. Clearly, her hitman had decided to leave the wreckage well alone. Maybe there was a fear of contaminating the scene, having anything traced back to him. He probably guessed that they would have enough explaining to do to hold them up without finishing his simple kill order. Or maybe he was just getting clear before his employer found out.

Whatever the reasons, Catriona simply grabbed her stuff, placed it in the back of the taxi, and sat there with Tiff. Inside of half an hour, they were in the main town, and had picked up a hire car ready to start driving towards Lichtenstein. As they sped along the back roads from Luxembourg, making their way south towards Lichtenstein, Catriona became aware that Tiff was staring at her.

'Are you all right?'

Of course, I'm not all right, thought Catriona. *Look at the mess we're in. How can she ask me if I'm all right?* 'No.'

'I'm sorry. I failed, didn't I?' Tiff put her head down and Catriona could hear some sobbing.

'You haven't failed, Tiff, and we haven't failed yet. We've still got this last address to go to.'

'But they have the jewels,' sniffed Tiff. 'They've got them all. I failed and you won't clear Luigi's name.'

Catriona pulled over to the side of the road, and turned to face her niece. 'First off, we've failed. This is a team effort.'

'Yes, but I'm the intelligent one.'

'This is a team effort. I don't care who's what. Secondly, we're still alive. Thirdly, we're not dead in the water yet. There's still this final address, so sniff your tears back in and focus. Feel the breeze from the drive and keep the brain turning over while I drive. Come on, Tiff. I need you.'

I do need you, Tiff. I'm at the end of exhaustion. I'm at the end of my talent. There's nothing left here, thought Catriona. *This last address is a shot in the dark. It's a next-to-nothing call. They're bound to have been there before. If they've got all the jewels, they've got what they wanted, and they can go and sell them, do what they want, and we'll never see any of it again, but Luigi's name will be mud. He's not a thief.*

'Do you think Luigi actually did do this, that he was involved?'

'Look,' said Catriona, pushing her hand into Tiff's. 'You didn't know Luigi. There was no one like him. So kind, so caring, wild too, prepared to run around and do whatever, but he was no thief. The only thing Luigi ever stole was my heart.'

'That's really cheesy,' said Tiff, staring out of the front of the car. 'I can't believe you said that.'

It was cheesy, wasn't it, thought Catriona. 'It's true as well and he did steal it.'

Gaston was a small village in Liechtenstein and on arrival, Catriona entered a nearby shop pointing to the address on a piece of paper. Through some rather strange directions and plenty of hand waving and finger pointing, Catriona realised that the address was on the edge of town, out into the country. Her contact had indicated it was some sort of eatery by pretending to shovel something into her mouth from a bowl. As Catriona had gone to leave the shop, the woman ran after her and tapped her on the shoulder. In some garbled French, Catriona believe she asked if Cat will be seeing her friends.

'What friends?' Cat replied in French.

'The ones that were here before. You might catch them. It's only been two hours.' Catriona's heart thumped. Had they really not got here much earlier after a couple of days travel? Catriona had reorganised and then travelled. Had that not been enough for them to conclude their business? She raced out of the shop, the woman waving and gesticulating good luck behind her. Catriona jumped behind the wheel and drove off, causing Tiff to fall backwards into her seat.

'Steady on. What's the rush?'

'They could be there. It's been two hours. The woman said it's been two hours since, "Friends of ours," have been here. Somebody asking for the same address.'

'Well, let's go then. Come on, put the foot down.'

Catriona could feel the sweat in her hands as she gripped the wheel throwing the car around corners. They were too tight for the speed she was doing. She remembered driving with Luigi in a Lamborghini, unable to control the power and spinning out on the corners of a test track in Italy. Luigi had laughed but he had not given up on her, and she spent the day with him continuing to practice. Cat thought she probably looked better draped over a car than she ever did driving around in it, but Luigi had been keen to help her to do the best she could. That was a thing about him. 'Slow into the corner,' she remembered, 'accelerate out of them. Be aware of the power of the vehicle.' Catriona laughed out loud causing Tiff to stare.

'There is no power in this vehicle, Tiff. There's just no power.' She saw Tiff's bemused look but Cat didn't care. She was lost in a good memory as she drove along that was causing her to be more daring as she took these corners with everything the car could muster. The road was tight and routing up a hill into a forest when Tiff shouted that a number matching the address was indicated at the side of the road. Catriona barely slowed down, swinging the car around and into a long track that seemed to serve as a driveway. Turning this way and that, she eventually arrived in a large car park beside a restaurant and a picturesque set of falls. Switching off the engine, Catriona stepped out and looked around.

There were two vehicles in the carpark. Neither were occupied and Cat watched Tiff walk over slowly, placing her hand on the bonnet of the cars. The restaurant was side on to them and before them was a gate leading to a wooden veranda beyond which the falls fell into a deep pool. *It's the sort of place Luigi would have liked. Spectacular foods and if the food is any good, it would have been perfect for him. But there's no one here,* thought Cat.

'Those engines are cold,' said Tiff. 'But look at the ground.' Cat saw her niece pointing to where the stones in the carpark had been shifted like a car had departed at speed. She saw two basic tracks and began to wonder what had caused somebody to leave in such a hurry.

'Stay close Tiff, we'll go and have a look.' Stepping towards the entrance of the restaurant, that was the small gate onto the veranda, Tiff heard the crash of the waterfall endlessly churning and caught a whiff of Alpine plants in the breeze. There was certainly a beauty about the place. She opened the small wooden gate and stepped through onto the broader veranda, looking first through the windows of the restaurant, but seeing no one. She was not that surprised for it was only ten o'clock in the morning. Maybe they would not open for another hour or so.

She gazed up at the waterfall, hidden in small trees that sat on the hillside. Looking down, she saw the water splash before a hideous site caught her eyes. On rocks below the veranda lay the body of a man. He was clearly dead. Bits of him had detached from the other part of the torso. As she looked deeper into the pool, trying to forget about the sight she'd just seen, she saw somebody floating face down.

'Tiff, stay very close. There's two dead down there.' She felt Tiff looking over her shoulder. Turning back to the restaurant, she saw the sign above it and the name, 'Weiss.'

'Well, we're in the right place,' said Catriona taking a step off the veranda up to the door of the restaurant. Pulling it back, she saw there were no lights on inside. Maybe the shift had only arrived when whatever incident had happened. There were many tables spread throughout the restaurant, none yet set or set up from the night before, chairs still stacked on them. There were no signs from the kitchen area when she could see into the rear of the building. The kitchen was one of those ones you could look through into, as if seeing people prepare your food would make it taste better afterwards. Catriona did not care. If you were somewhere like this, the food only had to taste good because the person opposite you should be what your eyes were looking at.

Tiff strode past Cat. She felt like she wanted to reach out for her niece and gingerly, she put her hand forward trying to bring Tiff back.

'There's no one here,' said Tiff. 'They've gone, that's what the tyre tracks are for, come on.' Tiff made her way to the kitchen, pulling open the door and looking inside. 'In here, there's someone on the floor, Cat.'

Catriona stepped into the kitchen as Tiff was pulling on some disposable gloves. She watched her niece bend down to start searching a man's pockets, the victim lying prostrate on the floor, two gunshots into his temple. To say there was a bit of mess behind his head would have been an understatement, but Cat thought that the word mess stopped her thinking any further about it. Tiff produced a wallet from inside the man's pocket and was now opening it, pulling out credit cards and the like. 'Jonas Weiss,' said Tiffany. 'It looks like he must have had something.'

'Put it all back the way you found it. We need to get a move on, get out of here.'

'Shouldn't we report this?' asked Tiff.

'And do what? How do we report this? What are you doing in a hire car in Liechtenstein? Oh, by the way, we hear that you went through Luxembourg. Were you with a group of nuns? You've been running around Copenhagen. Oh, and by the way, what happened on Mull? We don't want this trip to follow us, Tiff. We can't go back with anything until we know we can hand stuff over, and they've got it all. All the jewels have been taken, so what do we have, Tiff? What do we have? We have sorrow, sorrow.'

With that, Catriona bent over and began to cry. 'They'll think Luigi did it all. They'll think he was part of it, and then they'll think that I am just running around trying to tidy up. We can't do anything, Tiff. If we do, they could pin this on us. Pin it on you. These are bad people as well. We need to be kept out of it. We needed the jewels. We needed to be giving them back, and they're gone.'

'Maybe we could trace them somehow.'

'How, Tiff, how? People couldn't trace them for years.'

'But we've still got the burglary plans.'

'And that means what, Tiff,' said Catriona. 'Nothing, it means nothing. In fact, it probably implicates us, having the plans. There are next to no names. Oh, look, Weiss. That's that dead guy. Did you take that? All it shows is we know these people even though we don't.'

Cat wiped her nose, dried her eyes, and made her way out of the kitchen back to the veranda. She looked down into the pool, saw the bodies again, and instead turned and faced the waterfall.

She'd always loved waterfalls. She remembered Luigi waking her one morning from a chalet high in the Alps. She'd gone to have a shower and was about to get dressed, but instead, he threw his dressing gown to her and he walked her a short distance out to a waterfall that fell only some ten meters into a cold pool. She thought he was outrageous when he threw off his gown and dived in, but they were up in the middle of nowhere and so she had done the same.

She remembered now, he told her to stand there with the water cascading down on top of her head. The coolness racing across her skin had been exhilarating, but not as much as the smile on his face when she had opened her eyes to look at him. Maybe that is what this is all about. Keeping those memories as good times. Keeping them as cherished. She did not want to think of Luigi as having been a liar. Someone that had a hidden past that she did not know about. Maybe that's why Catriona was here. She needed to prove to herself that Luigi was no thief. She trusted him, didn't she? Hadn't she always? Was she now betraying him? She stood and watched the waterfall with tears streaming from her face. She could not stop them and part of her didn't want to.

'How about we go see your family?' said Tiff.

'Why in God's name would I want to go and see them? We left them to go on this quest, remember?'

'No, Cat, not your family. Your other family, Luigi's side.'

Cat burst out laughing, tears continuing to stream down her face. 'Why the hell would I want to see them? Tiff, they didn't want me. They threw me out. They chucked money at me, told me to go. They hated me. They thought he married beneath himself. Of all the people on earth who see me as a Contessa, it's not them. I'm a commoner, I'm muck, I'm nothing. What the hell are they going to do for me?'

'Well, they might know where he got the cobra's fang. After all, he never told you. He just presented it to you. Did it come from the family? Does it have a history? Is there anything we can trace back that we can find where these jewels came from? Maybe we can get the name of this woman who's run off with them. Maybe we can find out what really went on. The fang has got a story. All these jewels do. It starts at the bank, but the fang ends up with Luigi. We can't go to the bank and trace it, right? It's not safe. We don't want to be anywhere near the bank, but we can go to the people that knew Luigi. Love them or hate them, Cat, they know him, and they know his life before you.'

Catriona sniffed and wiped the tears off her eyes again. 'He didn't do it. He's not a thief.'

'I know he's not,' said Tiff.

'How?' spat Cat. 'How do you know? Don't just say things to please me.'

'I'm not,' said Tiff. 'I know he's not a thief.'

'How do you know?' asked Cat.

'Because you, you don't hang out with people like that. You were close with him, really close in a way I don't understand. He always said to me you did the social bit. You were good with the people. I don't think he could have hidden anything from you even if he'd wanted to. You read people too well, Auntie Cat. Too well.'

Catriona smiled, turned back to the waterfall, and thought of Luigi staring at her beneath it. 'You're right, Tiff, I do read people well. Let's go to Italy.'

'Of course, you don't always get me right,' said Tiff.

18

Chapter 18

Italian sunshine was always something Cat enjoyed. Now standing in the balcony of Luigi's ancestral home, she looked over the vineyards, and how the rays of the sun caressed the grapes that were beginning to grow. The family had their own winery, a label they were proud of, but the wine had never been to Cat's taste. She was more a woman for spirits and mixers, possibly a good cocktail as well. That was just one of several traits that the family disliked about her.

She had nearly spat out the first glass of wine they given her. It had not been her fault though. After all, it was so dry, it was ridiculous. It had not helped that Luigi had laughed, and his mother had stormed out of the room. The first meeting between the two women had gone badly, but it had not been the worst of it. The next couple of days, and a few more offensive comments and actions, had seen any chance of the two women coming together, and backing Luigi in life, as a very distant memory.

Instead, his mother had made it clear that Catriona was not

welcome anywhere. That night, Luigi had invited Cat down to dinner with the family and kissed her in front of them all declaring that this was a woman he would take on through this life. There were glasses smashed on the floor, they were disgusting comments made about her, but she had seen Luigi as her knight in shining armour—the man who would stand up before anyone declaring that she was his.

That had not happened much in her life. Usually, Catriona was used and discarded. 'Just another filly,' as one potential suitor had said, as if being compared to some sort of resource was a pleasing comment. Her own mother had heard that comment and said to Cat afterwards that she simply should have stood on the man's foot, turned round, and walked off in front of him. Catriona's effort of calling him a stallion, in the sense that he was like what hung between its legs, was not the sort of comment her mother appreciated. Although she did concede later that the guy was that sort of an idiot.

Tiff was bemused. When they had arrived, Catriona was well aware of all the formal graces and airs that would come. They would be invited to go and sit in the library, or the dining room, and they would have to wait for people to arrive. The servants would not look at them with disdain, just simply not look at them. There would be no smiles. There would be no personable interaction, and this nuance of an offended family was completely lost on Tiff.

'Did they just not have personalities? Are you not allowed? The staff, they just don't do anything, do they? They are like robots. Look at him over there, robot man. He's just like a robot.'

'They don't like me,' said Catriona, 'and because they don't like me, they won't like you. Because you're part of my family, you're part of me.'

'People are individuals,' said Tiff. 'Don't they get that?'

'Not here, they're not, and people aren't always individuals, Tiff. I'm not an individual. Luigi and me, we were a team. We still are a team.'

Cat watched her niece try to weigh up this comment. 'Don't even mention the fact he's dead. That doesn't stop you being a team.'

Tiff looked bemused, and then stood beside her aunt looking at the grapes. 'You think they could do more than just produce wine with all this money.'

'Like what?' asked Cat.

'You could put a whole load of refugees out there. You could build them little huts and stuff for them to live in until they can get proper homes. People with money need to do things.'

'But we haven't done anything. We've just basically run around the world holidaying. You seem quite all right with that.'

'Yes, but it's not my money, is it?' said Tiff. 'It's your money, you're the one doing it. I'm just keeping you company, looking after you.'

Cat smiled, and laughed into herself. *She is looking after me. I take her away to give her an opportunity in life and I'm being looked after by her.* Tiff's view of the world never stopped astounding Catriona.

The double doors to the balcony of the house opened. A manservant walked in announcing that the lady of the house would receive them in the drawing room. Cat walked inside. She was dressed in jeans, and she knew that Luigi's mother would be dressed up to the hilt. In fact, she probably spent the last hour or two getting herself ready, just so she could look the part beside Catriona.

Not that Catriona cared. They just needed to tell her some history, just needed to tell her where the cobra's fang had come from. The women descended through the house to the drawing room on the lower floor. With portrait after portrait gazing down on them, Luigi's family did not just have history. They seemed to own history in this part of the world.

'There's you,' said Tiff. Catriona was indeed up on the wall. She thought she looked like something from the sixteenth century. An elegant gown, ample cleavage, which for some reason, seemed to be a prerequisite on these pictures, but she was also aware that the picture of Luigi was not beside her. Instead, he was over towards the top of the stairs next to his brother.

'They did have one of the two of us,' Cat told her niece. 'I was darn good as well. I really rocked that—sort of Victorian-era wench in front of her man. I've got the figure for it, you see.'

'Women were certainly bigger in those days,' said Tiff. 'All over really.'

'Voluptuous, curvy,' said Cat.

'Bigger, fatter,' said Tiff. Her niece was so good at running you down just when you thought you had some decent attributes.

The manservant opened the great doors to the drawing room, thick oak structures with intricate carvings cut into them. When Catriona walked in, it was as if she was at home. There was no way she was going to grovel to this woman. After all, this was her home. Technically, she was the lady of the house; after all, Luigi's father had stepped down expecting Luigi to run the family business. He had done so, and therefore he was the Count. He was the man in charge.

Catriona was his good lady by his side, but they had never moved into the house. His mother never allowed it, so Luigi had decided never to stay there. In the whole time Catriona and he had been together, the only nights they'd spent here was in those early days, when the relationship between her and his family had fallen apart.

Catriona entered the drawing room and found Luigi's mother with her back to her. She knew that the woman wanted her to call out to say hello. She would wait and not turn around, waiting for Cat to come to the other side of her.

Catriona was not having any of this. Instead, she walked over to a small settee in the corner and sat down. She waved to Tiff to join her. The manservant stepped back out, closed the doors, leaving the three women in the room together. Five minutes of complete silence followed, broken only occasionally by Tiff gesticulating about what was going on.

Catriona would dismiss her with a wave, and Tiff would sit back down. After five minutes had passed, Tiff stood up and went to examine some books that were on the far side of the wall. Cat watched her slowly open an Italian geographical volume looking as if she was reading it intently. Then Tiff turned, closed the book, and slammed it onto the wooden floor.

Luigi's mother turned, fiercely jumping out of her seat, the diamond earrings flying around from her ears. She stared with venom at Tiff, crying out in Italian, 'Behave yourself, child.' She stormed over towards Tiff.

'Stop,' said Catriona. 'She is my guest. You will not speak to her like that. You've already insulted her by keeping your back to her. Since when did Luigi's house become a house of cold, a house where strangers are not welcome?'

'Depends who brings the stranger. You're not welcome.'

Catriona stood up and looked into the eyes of her mother-in-law. The woman stood at six foot, so much taller than Catriona, but she was a slimmer figure, more elegant than anything else. Catriona moved her shoulders back and allowed her fuller figure to come through as if this were some higher way of winning a competition.

'Sorry,' said Tiff. 'Dropped it. Who are you?'

Catriona nearly burst out laughing. Tiff had a wicked sense of humour, and she knew fine rightly who she was talking to.

'You'll have to forgive my niece. She has various issues, but kindly treat her with some respect. She does well to get on in this life.' Catriona was fully expecting Tiff to complain, but she saw she was working with Cat. Tiff stood and stared at Luigi's mother as if nothing were out of the ordinary.

'What do you want, and why are you back? We paid you money not to come. We paid you money to go away. Your staying in my son's life isn't enough without having to be back here again?'

'I need to know something. I need to know where Luigi bought me some jewellery.'

'What? No, no. If you have it, it should be back here. It belongs to us.'

'It does not,' said Catriona. 'It belongs to me. He wanted me, you understand that?'

'You scarlet hussy, charming him with what you have. You were nothing more than a body to him.'

'Oh, I was a body to him,' said Catriona, 'but I was so much more as well. He needed someone to be freer with, someone not to stifle him, someone not to—'

Luigi's mother slapped Cat across the cheeks. 'Don't you

speak of him like that. Don't you dare.'

The doors of the drawing room flew open, and in walked Luigi's brother. In many ways, he was like him, taller with a slightly more jutting chin. Cat always thought he looked quite dashing, but he did not have Luigi's joviality, a far more serious character despite being the younger brother.

'Do we have to have this? Did you have to come and upset her?'

'She was upset the day Luigi chose me,' said Cat. 'She never, ever got over that.'

'Get her out of here. Get her out of here. Francesco, take her away. I need to lie down. That's what she does to me. That's why she's not welcome here.' Francesco stepped across to Catriona, putting his arm around her back, trying to usher her out, but Cat stood her ground.

'This is still my home. You don't shove me about as if I'm the riffraff from the village.'

Francesco's face softened. 'Please, can we talk outside? You clearly want something; you won't get it from Mother. Come with me,' he whispered, 'I'll see what I can do for you.' Francesco led Catriona to the garden, inviting her to sit on a wooden bench with ornate handles on either end. Tiff sat beside her while Francesco stood looking out to the countryside.

'She misses him, you realise that, don't you? She misses him, and she was at war with him because of you.'

'It was never because of me. It was because of her and him. He chose what he wanted. She couldn't accept it. She wanted him to be something else.'

'She does control, but she's easier to handle when you're not here. You haven't helped me by coming back, Catriona. I know what he saw in you. I see it too, but we agreed. You weren't to come back. You have all the money you could need. Why are you here?'

'I need to know something about Luigi. There's been some issues. People are calling him things. He bought me a necklace, a sort of pendant, a jewel. It's called the cobra's fang. I need to know where he got it from, why it was given to me.'

Francesco looked out, basking in the sun, and the heat coming down on him. 'I don't know anything about that,' he said. 'When he took up with you, my brother didn't tell me much. He thought I would report it all back to Mother. That was not the case, but she could have got it out of me, I'll concede that. He was always able to resist her better than I did.'

'But the cobra's fang,' said Cat. 'I need to know about it. Who would know where he got it?'

'Alexandro, he knew everything.'

'But he's so quiet. I remember him from the wedding. He said so little. I could tell they were friends, but he just seemed to be a strong, stolid man. A lot less fun than Luigi.'

'You misjudge him,' said Francesco. 'Alexandro was as close to Luigi as you were, but he didn't show it the same. If there's secrets, Alexandro would know them, not me. He still lives up here, in the next valley, but I warn you, he's a man of honour. Luigi may have had secrets from you, and for good reason. Just be careful when you go to him. You may not like what you find out.'

'Do you know something?' asked Cat.

'I only know that my brother had secrets from me. Maybe he had them from you as well.'

'Looks like we need to go and see this guy,' said Tiff suddenly.

It was as if she had been part of the furniture, and had suddenly sprung to life, causing Francesco to be slightly shocked.

'Yes, we do, Tiff. We'll go there directly. Thank you, Francesco. Take care of her, she's too bitter for her age,' said Cat.

'That she is, Catriona,' said Francesco, stepping forward, placing his arms around Cat, holding her tight. 'I miss him too. We all miss him. I'm sorry you have to miss him alone.' Catriona squeezed tight, holding her brother-in-law close. She felt a tear in her own eye. When she stepped back, she saw one in his. 'And please, Cat, don't come back. You remind her of what she's lost.' Catriona nodded, and turned her back on her brother-in-law, making her way round to the front of the house.

'Charming family,' whispered Tiff.

'Luigi's family, Tiff; don't say what you're going to say. It's Luigi's family—don't speak ill of them.'

19

Chapter 19

Catriona had spent only the briefest time in the area where Luigi grew up, but in the late evening sunshine, the hills looked resplendent, and the vines that covered the area were plush with growing grapes. There was an obsession with wine in the area, one that Cat never shared. When she'd first come here with Luigi, she found the discussion about it boring, but the countryside with its old, vast, and impressive houses impressed her so much, that when she had to walk away from it all, a part of her had been deeply saddened.

The friend of Luigi she now sought, Alberto, had always been such a quiet person. When Luigi introduced Catriona to him, she always felt that he was overawed by her. Many times, she would catch him watching her, not in any perverted way, more in admiration. In every meeting he was pleasant, if somewhat quiet, and she would always find it difficult to understand how he had been the perfect foil to Luigi. Her husband had always spoken highly of him, said that he trusted him with everything, and now she wondered just what she could learn if what she wanted was being held in confidence.

Climbing up the winding path to a large estate house in the middle of an orchard of vines, Catriona felt somewhat underdressed. Despite having arrived at Luigi's family home dressed in jeans and jumper, she felt this was somehow inadequate for someone who was effectively only a passing friend to her. She had not got to know Alberto well. Most of what she knew had come from Luigi's own lips. Somehow, she'd have to connect with the man, forge a path of friendship that she never managed when Luigi was there.

Knocking on the large wooden doors at the front of the house, Catriona stepped back. She had hoped Tiff would be standing with her, but her niece had waited in the car, somewhat overawed by the vast scene in front of her, and maybe a bit anxious after the frosty reception from Luigi's mother.

One of the large wooden doors opened, and a butler stepped out, nodding politely and inquiring in Italian who Catriona was seeking. On advising him that she was looking for the master of the house, he said he was out for the evening. Cat declared it was a bit of an emergency, and to do with her former husband, Luigi.

The name clearly made an impression on the man, and he advised Cat that Alberto was down in the village at one of the restaurants in the main street. Thanking the man, Cat made her way back to the car, and drove through the pleasant evening light to the small village that serviced the need of all the surrounding mansions.

After inquiring at the given restaurant, Catriona found that Alberto had moved on, and was probably in one of the many bars along the main street of the village. Cat was undeterred by this, the village not being that large, and only having around three drinking establishments. It was settled deep within woods, carved out along three main roads that ran into it from the north, the south, and the west.

The buildings were old, showing signs of crumbling décor here and there, but if you looked at the architecture, it had once been fabulous. This had been a place of money, and still remained so, even if to keep up the more decadent touches these days was beyond the reach of the area.

Catriona walked along the street with Tiff in tow, muttering about having to be out amongst people. The girl said she was hungry. Cat eventually stopped, turned, and pointed to a restaurant, handing her some cash.

'Have your meal. Wait for a bit. If I'm not back, go to the car. I will make it back and be prepared to drive. I might have to become a bit more friendly with this.'

Tiff raised her eyebrow. 'I won't be carrying you anywhere. Keep your head. You don't know who else is about.'

'Stop worrying. The people that were after the jewels have got them. We don't know them. We know nothing. They couldn't care less about us now. But if Alberto doesn't know anything, I'll not know anything,' said Cat. 'He was Luigi's closest ally, his best friend. That could be the hard bit, getting him to tell me anything of note.'

Cat strode off, making her way across the cobbles at the town. At the edge of the village, she looked up and noted the sign, 'Vincente's.' She wondered if his daughter was still running the place. It hadn't been that long after all, but Cat doubted she would remember her. Luigi had been a patron all his life, and that's why she reckoned Alberto would be here.

She remembered her few evenings down in the village, and

she'd asked about the other drinking establishments, and been told quite abruptly at times, 'No, we drink in Vincenti's.' Had it all changed with Luigi's death? Had he been the one who wanted to go there? She would find out soon enough.

Inside the bar was fabulously gloomy, harking back to almost a medieval feel. The lit candles only enhanced that effect. The tables were wooden—the chairs too, but their roughness belied a quality of build, plus these chairs had come from good stock. The people that drank here should pay over the odds, and therefore they expected furniture that was not only atmospheric, but also perfectly functional.

There was an occasional tapestry on the wall, and behind the bar she saw a familiar wave of brown hair. Vincente's daughter never liked to tie it up. It would always swing when she arrived with the drinks. She ran a tight bar, an impressive woman in her own right, but she took no nonsense. Many a young man had thought they could get cute with her, possibly wheel her off for a night of passion. Each had left with a foot up his backside, sprawling on the cobbles outside. It was almost a rite of passage for those who had too much money and thought that power came easily. Fortunately, none of Luigi's friends were like that and hence they were welcomed at the bar.

The woman turned round and Catriona saw instant recognition, but there was no song and dance, merely a faint smile, and then a flick of the head indicating Catriona should be looking in the far corner. Of course, that was always their corner. Cat nodded her thanks and made her way quietly to where a single candle sat in a dark alcove. There were murmurs from those drinking at the tables around her. Cat was not dressed for this bar. You should look classy. In this world they would think nothing of it if someone marched in wearing a large ball gown, or one of today's modern expensive suits. Whatever you wore, it had to be classy, and the one thing Catriona was not at the moment was a model of high fashion. Her jeans were not designer, and neither was the jumper, but she'd had to purchase them on the run.

Cat could hear their chatter from the alcove, some raucous laughing, all male voices. It must have been a night for the boys. Luigi had gone on those occasionally, and she knew it was healthy even though she hadn't established any female friends by that point. He had asked if she would let him go, and of course she did, for there were many other times when she was happily brought into this crowd.

As she stood beside the table, she saw a cigar being lit. A young man leaned back, staring at her intently while blowing out the smoke he had just inhaled. Cat did not recognise him, but instead moved round the group of gentlemen, some six in number. There at the rear was Alberto. The man was squat, as small as Cat herself, and had a face that many would have said was closed, but his eyes looked up, and she saw the recognition.

'Give us a moment,' he said to those around him in Italian, and she believed many of them must have realised who she was for they departed, giving a humble nod as they walked past her.

'I thought they said you shouldn't come back. They chased you away.'

'They tried, but this is Luigi's home. It's good to see you, Alberto.'

'It always was good to see you. Come and sit. Tell me how you've been getting on. It can't have been easy without him.' Catriona slid her way round the table, sitting next to Alberto. 'You know I was always jealous of him, don't you?'

Cat looked up into the man's barely-lit face. She was trying to gauge whether he was kidding or not. It was a handy complement to throw out, whether he meant it or not. The men in these parts could throw you compliments without meaning one word of it. His hand went up and touched her cheek. 'It is really good to see you. He was most fortunate. I was jealous of him. Truly.'

'No,' said Cat, 'I never knew that. You were always this quiet one, his companion, loyal, faithful.'

'If I hadn't have been,' said Alberto, 'I may have tried to steal you from under his nose. You look like you've come on hard times,' he laughed. 'Still, you can look good in whatever you're in. I always thought that.'

'I need your help. I need to know something about Luigi.'

'I knew you would be here for something. It would not be a social visit. You and his mother, you couldn't be in the same place on a social visit.'

'Well, she wasn't exactly happy to see me. Neither was his brother.'

'That's unfair,' said Alberto. 'He has to keep the peace up there. That's why he made you the deal. You lack for nothing, do you?'

'Only Luigi,' said Cat, 'but that can't be helped. I need you . . . I need you to tell me if Luigi ever spoke to you about the cobra's fang.'

Cat watched the man shrink back suddenly. 'No, nothing at all.' It was clear he was lying. Something had shocked him, rocked him about this.

Catriona placed her hand on Alberto's. 'It's important. I need to understand something. It's been stolen. I've chased all the way across Europe trying to find it. They said he was a thief, Alberto. They've labelled Luigi as a thief, and I'm getting labelled with it as well. The police said he stole it—or at least he and a group of people—from an Italian bank. There are several other pieces. There's a panda, a crane, a group of jewels altogether that must have been taken from the bank. Why would Luigi steal from a bank?'

'I can't tell you but know this. He was not a thief. He did it for good reason.'

'Well, then, tell me,' said Catriona, sliding closer to the man.

Alberto put his hands on Catriona's shoulders, and looked straight into her eyes. 'He made me promise not to tell you. He never wanted you to know.'

'Know what?'

'I shouldn't say. Even though he's dead, it was a promise made to him.'

'But if you hold that promise, his name will be mud. They may even come and look at me about my involvement. Alberto, I've had a gun put to my head several times. People who quite simply don't want me involved. I think they may still come after me.' This part was a lie, and Catriona felt bad inside for doing it, but this was her last hope. She knew she needed the answer.

'I swore to him that I would always help you; I'd always protect you if anything ever happened to him. It was I who pushed Francesco to give you the money, to give you a lifestyle, even though it was yours already to take. I guess he might forgive me. It was back here though you might not remember. We were sat at this very table on a night out, and there was a gentleman come around, although he was no gentleman. You complained to Luigi because the man kept staring at you. He even came up and rubbed your neck.

'That creep,' said Cat. 'He had hands like anything. I told Luigi, and the next thing, the man had disappeared. Luigi had stepped outside to him. What's it got to do with him?'

'That creep was a son of a count, and their family has always been in competition with Luigi's over the years. You weren't here long enough to see the full effect of it when it happened. Things sometimes got bitter, but that man took a liking to you. He told Luigi so in no uncertain terms. Told him he would have his English whore.'

'I'm not English,' said Cat, and then something else in her head wondered why she'd pick that side of the statement, and not the other one. Surely the main offense came from the other word.

'And you're nothing of the sort, which is why Luigi took him outside, and challenged him to a duel. You may remember Luigi wasn't around the following morning, and neither was I. They fenced with swords, Luigi putting him to the ground, holding a sword at his neck. He should've finished him. The man deserved it, but Luigi was no butcher. Instead, he demanded a prize from him, a prize for his life, and the man gave Luigi the cobra's fang. Luigi didn't really know what it was, but he knew he wanted you to wear it. He knew he wanted you to be on his arm in front of the man, wearing that necklace, so he understood exactly who you were.'

'And who's that?'

'A lady of class and distinction, the Contessa, Luigi's Contessa. No one else's. But of course, he didn't want you to know he'd been fighting in a duel. Didn't want you to know that side of him, and so he swore to me that I was not to tell anyone. Made me promise. Said I was to protect you through all things, and I swore it, and I was jealous as anything of him.'

'Then I need to go and see him, this count's son. You need to tell me all about him, for I need information from him. I fear he may have besmirched Luigi's name.'

'And I shall tell you, but you shall not go this evening. You shall stay with me,' said Alberto. 'Stay here, drink and talk. I told you I was jealous of him. Jealous over you, but I was honourable, always, Catriona. Always honourable to the Contessa, and I still shall be, but tonight, you shall talk to me. For once, Luigi shall not steal you away. Sit and talk with me about him, about you, about everything.'

Alberto raised his hand in the air. Catriona saw Vincente's daughter pick up a couple of bottles of wine. There would be no going to this new part of the mystery tonight. Instead, she would talk with an old friend like she had never talked before, and inside, Catriona was happy with that. Since her husband's death, there had been no one to talk to about Luigi. No one who really knew him. Even Tiff, for all the boon that she had been, she could never reminisce like Alberto would be able to.

She watched him pour the wine. They chinked the glasses, and Catriona drank half her cup in one go. She was due this. God bless, Alberto.

20

Chapter 20

Catriona's head hurt although she was driving the car. She had both windows rolled down, desperately trying to get some fresh air through her lungs to clear out the cobwebs that had formed in her mind. She could feel Tiff's annoyance beside her. The girl had eventually found her at around one a.m., still sitting with Alberto, laughing. They had found some rooms in the village around two, organised by Alberto hauling an old friend up from his bed. Then at eight o'clock, they had risen.

Alberto had left a route to follow, to find the man who had insulted Cat, who had insulted Luigi and suffered for it. Salvatore was his name, and Cat was determined to meet him. She only wished that she had the cobra's fang on her. She would wear it with pride, putting it right into his face. Last night, Alberto had told of the jewel, of how Luigi had mocked the man when he knocked him to the ground. Alberto said he had never seen such anger in Luigi, and he knew then that Catriona was to be the special one. 'For no man defends a woman like that unless she holds that place in his heart.' He said that was the point when he had stepped back as a friend, had let his own feelings for her subside away. Although her head now hurt, a lot of feelings had been exorcised last night, a lot of sorrows had been borne up together and bared to each other's soul so that now they were more at peace.

'Are you sure you know where you're going?' said Tiff.

'No. You have the map, Alberto's map. Look at it and just tell me if I'm on the wrong path.'

'I can't make head or tail of this. Half of it's in Italian.'

'Give it here,' said Cat, pulling it across, placing it on the steering wheel and then looking at it, desperately trying to focus. Her eyesight was fine, but at the moment, she was struggling to focus on the road, never mind the piece of paper several inches from her face. 'It's a little further, Tiff. Don't worry. We will get there.'

Tiff was tapping her feet for the rest of the journey, and Cat knew she was just waiting to point out that they hadn't arrived at their destination. But when they swung up to a large group of trees, drove for half a mile up the side of a mountain, then had arrived at an impressive chateau, Tiff's foot stopped tapping.

The grounds of this particular mansion were impressive, and the turrets around the top of the building left Catriona in awe. There was something so terribly ostentatious about it and terribly different from Luigi's own home. There was a grandeur here, something that spoke of time past, something Luigi would never be a part of. He had been a modern man, but this spoke of family, and of tradition and history.

As Catriona pulled up in the hire car in the gravel driveway that had wound through the impressive gardens, she saw an angry man running out. He had an apron around him and looked as if he was a cook or manservant, but with his hands he was making a shooing action and was telling the women in Italian that this was not a tourist hotspot. They should return to the road and leave. This was private land.

Cat opened the car door and stepped out, walked round to the front of the car, placed her hands on her hips as the man came right up before her. He was taller than her by several inches, and she had to look up into his face. For a minute, he gave a diatribe about tourists and how they were a pain, ruining the place, getting in the way, knowing nothing of where they stood.

Catriona saw Tiff almost cowering in the car. She was out of her comfort zone here in a world she didn't really know, and that meant she would hide away, hide behind Catriona, which was fine because Catriona did know where she was. More than that, she knew who she was. She placed a finger on the man's lips.

'I am the Contessa de Los Palermo. Tell your master I am here. I wish to see Salvatore, and I want to see him now.'

Catriona wondered what sort of figure she cut in her jeans and large jumper. She was travelling extremely light, still wearing the same clothes from the day before. Her hair was a little unkempt, but probably only so much so that she would notice it. But with her hands on her hips, she hoped she cut an impressive figure. The man stood and stared at her.

'You are no Contessa. You've read that from a brochure,' the man called at her in Italian.

'Do you mock a widow? I'll see you on the streets for this.' With that, Catriona reached up and slapped the man across the cheek. 'Take me to Salvatore and open the door for my niece.'

The man was simply stunned, but Cat knew that the arrogance with which she'd done it could only come from those who thought themselves in a higher position. The man would understand this, the treatment, the way she was looking down her nose at him. Of course, it was all an act. This was not Cat, but this was a Contessa, and the man understood. Quickly, he ran to the car, opening the door, and then stood rather embarrassed as Tiff sat there, not flinching from the passenger's seat.

'Tiff, get out. We're going to see the man.' Once her niece had decided to exit the vehicle, the man took them up to the front double doors banging loudly, until the butler arrived. He explained in Italian to him that this was the Contessa de Los Palermo, and Cat caught the look of the butler, almost of one of disgust, but she marched up to the man and demanded to see Salvatore right then.

'I'm afraid he is indisposed at this time. He is currently with a guest. I suggest you make an appointment.'

With that, Cat stepped forward and pushed the man to one side, marching into an impressive hall space. Large wooden doors swept away from it, and before her was a large marble staircase. For a moment, she thought to herself, where would she go? She had traipsed in like a woman with purpose, and now she simply looked lost. She would have to take a chance. With a guest they had said and so she marched up the stairs.

'Where are you?' she shouted. 'Where are you, Salvatore? The English whore is here.' Cat rounded the top of the stairs, arriving on the first floor of the house. She marched along the corridor followed by Tiff and a panicking butler behind her. The man was crying out in Italian telling her she should wait, that he would get the master, but Cat was having none of it. She barged along the hallway. A door opened before her, and a man stood in a silk dressing gown. He was slightly older than when she'd first met him. Indeed, his face was just a hazy image, but this was he. This was Salvatore. A head popped out behind the door Salvatore had emerged from—a blonde-haired woman who he snapped at to get back into the room. He was indeed attending to a guest.

'The Contessa,' he said, smiling at Catriona, 'and in such feisty mood. No wonder he liked you.'

Catriona marched up to the man. 'Get dressed, get downstairs, because I need to talk to you. If you don't, God help me, I'll run my sword through your neck where my husband didn't.'

Catriona hoped she was striking fear into the man. She saw a nervousness in him that delighted her and turned on her heel making for downstairs. As much as she saw a hint of fear in the man's eye, she also heard him speak under his breath. It was in Italian, and maybe he did not know just how much Italian she understood. The English equivalent would have been, 'Fine filly,' or a similar disparaging thought about a woman. It seemed Luigi's sword had done him no good.

Tiff was rather pleased with herself, sitting on a large, comfortable sofa and stuffing some croissants down her throat. Catriona was too angry to eat. This was where she would finally realise where the jewel had come from. It was an important moment, because if this man could not provide them with anything, their quest to clear Luigi's name would be gone. The butler had desperately tried to make amends for his attitude earlier, bringing coffee and breakfast, but it was a good twenty-five minutes before Salvatore ghosted into the room as if nothing had happened at all.

'Contessa, such a delight to see you again. I was so sad to hear of your husband's demise.' The man stepped forward to take Catriona's hand and to place a kiss on it, but Catriona pulled it back.

'Let's not pretend that we are somehow friends. I know what he did to you. As for me, he should've run you through. I'm only here because I need something from you, something you're going to tell me. The jewel you gave him, the cobra's fang—where did it come from?'

Salvatore seemed stunned. 'Why?'

'Because it's gone,' said Catriona. 'Somebody came to my house and took it, a jewel given to me by Luigi, a jewel that spoke of his respect for me, dispatching someone who saw only an English whore. Where did you get it from? Why have people come to my house?'

Salvatore seemed to shake inside. He stumbled backwards, collapsing into a chair. 'You're not the first to ask of that, not recently. There was a blonde-haired woman, came up to me. She drank with me. I thought she was probably going to come home with me. She steered the conversation towards things I had done in the past, dangerous things.'

'What do you mean by that?' asked Catriona. 'What does that mean?'

'I'd taken on certain commissions, more for a lark. I don't need the money, but you have to keep entertained, don't you?' said Salvatore. 'One of my friends, he got wind of a man who wanted something. It was in the Italian bank in Milan. He said it couldn't be done, but I funded it. I funded all the people just for a laugh. We were asked to steal them, a collection of jewels little known but worth an awful lot, especially to private collectors. You or Luigi wouldn't have known anything about them, not what they were worth.'

'You stole them for whom, though? You said you took a commission.' Tiff had suddenly put her croissant down and was listening intently to what the man had to say.

'You would probably call him a crime lord. "Mafia," people would say if they didn't understand the area. This man isn't that, but he is as dangerous. He had all the contacts to get me all the schematics, and I broke in with my four friends. We did it, too. When I saw the jewels and I thought of handing them to him, no one would ever know. No one would ever know we did it, that I masterminded it. So, we told them we failed. Sure, we got them out of the bank, but we had to ditch them.

'He came with his people. He couldn't find them at all. We were threatened, but he could find nothing. My father has great influence, and he wouldn't dare strike against us. He's a powerful man but not that powerful. My father would wreak vengeance, hire people to go after him, but I carried it on me. The cobra's fang, that was mine, my part to take. The rest went to my friends. They took them—Weiss, Clausen, Mertens, and Jones.'

'We've met a few of them,' said Tiff, 'but how do they know? How did these people know you had them?'

'What's the point of it to you,' said Salvatore standing up, 'unless you can back it up? I had lost my jewel. Your husband's sword saw to that. It was the only thing I had on me of value I could offer him for my life. But the others, they would talk, especially Mertens. Belgians like to boast, do you not think so? Maybe you haven't got the experience of the different European cultures. You English don't listen anyway. You don't learn. It's like a separate history over there.'

'So, the crime boss, the one from this area, do you think he's got wind of it? You think he knows?' asked Tiff.

'I told the others I'd lost mine, and I told him, the others had them. Sounds like he came for his goods.'

'He came for everybody else except you,' said Catriona.

'You said you were approached by a woman,' asked Tiff. 'What did she look like?'

'She was blonde, a still look in her eye, very beautiful in her own way. Not as feisty as you, Contessa, more professional in demeanour. I hope that doesn't offend you.'

'You have offended me, my husband, and the family more than enough for a lifetime. I am beyond your offense, but you can tell me where this crime boss lives. Tell me his name and his location, and then you can shut up and say nothing for the next month to anyone about me, or my niece, or about the cobra's fang.'

'What makes you think you can hold anything over me?' said Salvatore.

This caused Catriona to rise to her feet, and she marched over to the man, placing a finger on his chest. 'Luigi never spoke of the jewel. Alberto didn't either. It was kept between them, kept away from the public. In fact, you're the only one who mentioned it, because you lost the *fang*. You don't stay silent, and I'll make sure everyone knows it. Your family, Luigi's family, the whole area, they'll know of how you spoke to the Contessa de Los Palermo and of how her count put a sword to your throat. You'll be a laughingstock. That's why you won't speak. You can write down the address and the name of this crime boss. Have your butler deliver it to our car out at the front. My niece and I will be there.'

Catriona turned on her heel and made her way to the door of the room they were in. As she opened it, she turned back round, 'For your information, I'm not English, I'm Scottish. And I'm not feisty; I'm simply pissed.'

21

Chapter 21

Catriona sat looking out of the car, up at the large mansion on the hill. The address she'd been given had led to this large-seeming fortress, the entire grounds surrounded by a high security fence and guards walking here and there along the perimeter. Someone was obviously worried about their enemies and Cat quickly realised she was not going to get inside the house without a small army. Instead, along with Tiff, she drove back and forward, trying to keep an eye on the comings and goings, but now on the third day of staking out the mansion, she was becoming disheartened.

'Maybe we could break-in, like at night time,' said Tiff. 'If we donned up our garb, I could try and take out the electrics at one of the gates, go in that way.'

'Stop,' said Cat. 'This isn't some little house in the main street; look at it. There's no way we are going to be able to break in there, and if we do and we get caught, we're dead. I'm not risking you on that. It's better to wait and look for another opportunity.'

'You don't trust my skills, do you?'

'Against that? Frankly, Tiff, no. Don't get me wrong; you've done some really good work at times but that's way beyond you. We'd need some sort of government agent with us.'

Tiff shuffled in the passenger seat and stared up at the large mansion, and the backdrop of the mountainside behind it gave it almost an evil lair look. Catriona was reminded of the cartoons she had watched when younger. She had not met this crime boss, whoever he was, and maybe she didn't want to. Did he appear with a large cloak behind him, like the villains in those cartoons? Not being able to see him kept the mystique going.

She had thought of asking around the place, checking out the local villages and towns, seeing what people knew about him, but at the moment, she doubted he knew that they were there and that was key. If he took an interest in them, if he saw them as some sort of a threat, no matter how little, he might just squash the bug on his windscreen.

'Shall we drive round to the back gate again, go past there? It's got that viewpoint, hasn't it?'

'No,' said Cat. 'We don't stop at the viewpoint; we stopped there twice already. If we get the same guard on the gate, he's going to get suspicious, but we'll drive past.' Cat had taken the precaution of changing the hire car twice now, and she had purchased a scarf, which she'd wrapped around her head the second time they'd passed by. As much as she wanted to clear Luigi's name, she was aware that she could not do much if she were dead. Maybe this would be a long game, she did not know. What had surprised her was the lack of messages from Tiff's father. Her brother, whilst never one to check up on Catriona, did at least have some sort of affection for his daughter, but clearly with her out of the way now, he was enjoying himself.

Cat had asked Tiff if she had had any communication from him, but Tiff wouldn't be bothered either way. She was on the case, and the case came first.

The women drove the winding road up the side of the mansion grounds, and as they passed the side gate, they saw a car emerging. It was more of a small van, the rear without windows, and Cat wondered what sort of deliveries it brought. She had visions of drug running, the van piled high with white powder. Maybe that was just fantasy; after all, why would you do that on your own doorstep? Surely the organisation would have places by waterfronts for that, underground lairs. Cat realised that she was getting quite fantastical about this person she had never met.

'That's the third time that thing's come out,' said Tiff, almost nonchalantly.

'That's what, Tiff?'

'The third time in three days that vehicle's come out. Some sort of routine drop-off. Maybe we could follow it and then we can impersonate them, get in that way?'

Catriona thought this was a crazy idea but at the moment, she had no ideas what to do about advancing her plan forward to recover her jewels.

'Okay, we'll follow it but at a distance. We'll not get overexcited about it.' Now having passed the side entrance, Catriona pulled over, got out of the car, and opened the boot, fumbling inside for something. When she saw the van drive past, she stepped back, shook her head in case anyone was watching, closed the boot, jumped back in the car, and drove after the van. She was keeping a reasonable distance and as it was not speeding, she was able to keep a matching speed with it.

This was as much distraction for Tiff as anything else and she doubted they would get anything from it, but maybe they would end up in the village, stop, and have some lunch. It was getting near that time. The road wound along the mountainside and then dropped towards a valley. The lush mountainside shone in the sun and Cat felt upset that she never really got to spend a lot of time here in Italy, in Luigi's backyard. They followed the car down into the village at the centre of the valley and watched as it parked up beside a river. From out of the rear of the vehicle, a man climbed out, dressed in a dapper suit. He must have been sixty, maybe sixty-five. He had a light scar on one side of his face. As he got out, a man stepped out of the passenger seat of the van and followed him at close quarters.

Cat had pulled the car over, parking it at the side of the street. She leaned over to Tiff who seemed engrossed in the man. 'Don't focus on him so intently; we'll get out and follow but we need to look like tourists. The way you're staring, you might as well have a magnifying glass up to your eye: Look at me, I'm Sherlock Holmes.'

'I know what I'm doing,' said Tiff, and opened the car door, stepping out. Cat followed her, and they trailed the man along the street before seeing him turn right into a restaurant. The restaurant backed onto the river that ran through the valley. Cat decided that rather than follow him into the restaurant, they would look for some way to walk along the riverbanks. It did not take long to find a small alley that cut through and then joined the path along the riverbank.

Cat tried to count along how many houses and premises were ahead of them to see if the man could be seen through any of the windows, but as she reached the riverbank and crossed a small bridge to the other side, she was able to see a large eating area at the rear of the restaurant, and the man was seated at a table.

Cat grabbed Tiff's arm. 'Let's get off the path. Get up into these bushes. We can watch from there.' Tiff nodded and the pair cut in through a thicket. Cat found her hair being pulled at, but she made no noise, instead dragging herself through and outwardly cussing about how her hair was being messed up by this thorny bush. Only once she found a comfortable spot, did she stop and stare across the riverbank.

The man was seated at a table on his own, and the gentleman who had got out of the vehicle with him was a few tables away. Cat had a feeling that this may have been him, the crime boss, the one who had looked for the jewels from the Italian bank in the first place, who had got the crazy Count's son to take on the job, and who had then been lied to.

'It's not easy to see from here. He's so far away,' said Cat. Immediately, a pair of small binoculars appeared in front of her face.

'You have to be ready for things like this. Someone trained like me hasn't got a problem, but I can see an amateur, like yourself, would struggle. He's on his own now. It looks like he's having some sort of red wine.'

'He's not on his own for long,' said Cat.

'Why? I can't see anybody with him.'

'Just came in, Tiff. You recognise her?' Tiff looked over, and Cat heard the gasp from her niece as a blonde-haired woman entered the restaurant. Cat recognised her as the one who had ordered the women to be killed and an anger built up inside her. She was the one who had caused all this bother. She was the one who had hunted down the cobra's fang.

'Do you think she knows him?' asked Tiff. Cat watched the woman walk across the restaurant, and the man stood up, unbuttoning his double-breasted jacket. He embraced her and the two kissed like there was no one around.

'I think he knows her,' said Cat. 'I only wish I could hear what they were saying. You don't have any of those things, you know, the little umbrellas with the microphones at the front?'

'A sound listening device to record what they say?'

'Yes, Tiff. One of those.'

'No,' said Tiff, shaking her head, putting the binoculars back up to her eyes and staring intently at the scene.

Bastard, thought Cat. *We finally get him; he's talking to a woman we know who's heavily involved, but I can't hear what they've said. If only there was some way of knowing where she's put the jewels. Does she still have them? Was she going to hand them over to him? She'd entered the restaurant with nothing in her hands, no bag, and was wearing a light blouse and skirt. She didn't look like she was here for business, more like entertainment.*

Cat watched the pair. They seemed very convivial in each other's company, hands occasionally went across the table, and despite being maybe twenty to thirty years younger than the man, she seemed to enjoy his company. This didn't seem like a business transaction, but it must be surely. If only she had been able to hear what they were saying.

'This is frustrating, Tiff, isn't it? I mean, they're right there barely one hundred yards from us, and we don't know what's going on. We finally get him out of his mansion, finally get to see the guy. His main co-conspirator comes along with him, and we can't even hear what they're saying.'

'Shh,' said Tiff, 'I'm concentrating.'

'That's it, Tiff, you stare away. What are you going to learn about after all?'

'She's going to do the drop tomorrow,' said Tiff.

'What?' said Cat, almost stumbling, catching the side of her face on a thorn, causing her to stifle a yelp.

'I told you, they're going to do the drop tomorrow.'

'How do you know that?'

'I can read his lips. He just said it and I think it's here. It's here, there's going to be a boat on the river, they're going to drop the jewels onto the boat, and he's going to squirrel them away somewhere. I didn't get where he was going with them. He's well-pleased with her. That's what he said. I think they're meeting up in a week's time somewhere.'

'Did he say where?'

'Somewhere in the Alps, I think. Got a bit harder to read then. It's definitely the jewels. I'm sure he said the word *fang* as well.'

Catriona's eyes lit up, 'Did they say here? You're sure they said here?'

'Lunch. That's what he said. Lunch again, right here.'

'Then that's our chance, Tiff. That's our chance. You're absolutely sure about this?'

'I keep telling you, I know how to do this—you don't. I wish you really would just listen to me.'

Catriona stared across at the restaurant, watched the man and the woman tucking into their meal. She would bring the jewels tomorrow into the restaurant, they'd do a switch, and would go on to a boat. They would need to be there. Cat and Tiff would need to be there. If they could grab and run, that would work. Dress up somehow.

'Tiff, get a good look at the waitresses and waiters around there. Look at the uniform. We might need to copy it. I'm going to need to formulate a plan about what we do here.'

'You're thinking you're just going to walk into the restaurant and just take it from right under their nose?'

'I'm thinking that, Tiff. That's exactly what I'm thinking. The only part I haven't worked out yet is how I'm going to get away.'

22

Chapter 22

The next day was a hot one, much to Catriona's annoyance. They'd spent the previous day searching the villages for clothes similar to the uniforms worn by the restaurant staff. It was simple, something black for the women, but as per usual, Catriona was struggling to get her size. The hard part was when she'd rounded up the clothes for serving in, she then needed an outfit over the top that didn't look like she was wearing something that could accommodate an Arctic winter. Despite this, she had found a long skirt that would cover the trousers of the uniform. A stylish jacket also meant the black over top would not be seen. A simple scarf around her neck hid her paleness, and she tied her hair up under a hat.

Tiff had given the note of approval commenting about disguises and insisted that Catriona put on more makeup than she ever had before. Cat wasn't one for makeup. If you needed too much of it, you were on a loser already. It was there to highlight, to bring out what you had. At this moment, as she sat at a table in the restaurant having ordered a salad, she felt like she had a layer of cake on her face.

It was decided that Catriona would do the snatch, basically because whoever was making the grab would have to be inside the restaurant. They'd be dressed up as a waitress, and Cat was the only one with good Italian. She could converse with the best of them and her accent, according to Luigi, was pretty reasonable. However, she was struggling to keep her hands from shaking, and she held them underneath the table.

Across from her, approximately four tables away, was the man in a silver suit. Again, he looked dapper, but this time, his suit was brighter. He also had a jovial cravat on. Cat thought he almost looked excited. Was it at the thought of the jewels? Was it at the thought of the woman coming again? She didn't know, but then she looked beyond him and saw Tiff walking along the far side of the riverbank.

The plan was that Cat would snatch the jewels and then possibly throw them across to Tiff. Cat would jump off the outdoor paved area of the restaurant, down to the riverbank, and fling the items over before running away, to make for a hire car they had parked in the village. Tiff would run off in a different direction. Hopefully, they might be able to do the switch between the two of them without anyone seeing.

It was a very ad hoc plan, one that was going to have to work on the hoof. They had no idea how the jewels were coming, if it'd be in a briefcase or a simple bag, or maybe the woman would be wearing them.

There was no way of knowing, and therefore, Cat felt she was missing that part of the movie, the one where the plans were all detailed out. It was always easy in the movies. It's always in that montage of people moving through the grand scheme and intercut it with the planning sequence. Everyone always seemed very happy that everything would work out, but as Tiff had said the previous evening whilst running over the plan, she was aware of the large holes in the scheme, and they were not overly sure about what to do with the jewels after.

How could they get them back to the Italian bank? They could be on the run for a while. Did they just drop them into a police station? Could the local police station be trusted? Cat had heard of corruption in police forces and, while she had no evidence that any of the local officers were on the take, she neither knew of any of them she could trust.

Cat picked at her salad and then saw the man in a silver suit stand up. His arms were wide, and he was smiling, shouting across to the blonde-haired woman who had just entered the restaurant. 'Victoria, Victoria,' he cried and then told her she looked like a goddess as she made her way across the restaurant.

He was clearly Italian, his accent from the local area, but when the woman replied, Cat thought she was not a local, or even Italian. The woman had a small handbag and was dressed in a skirt that stopped at the knees. Her blouse was full, and she was showing plenty of neckline as she elegantly walked across the restaurant and took the man's embrace. Before she sat down, he produced something from his pocket, and placed a necklace around her.

'Time to eat,' said the man, clicking his fingers. Cat watched a waiter rush desperately over to him. The couple ordered wine and then browsed the menus as if they were simply out for a working lunch. Most of the chatter, from what Cat could hear, was about skiing the Alps, and part of her began to wonder, did she miss something the day before? But with all this secrecy, it must be him. Why else would he be disappearing out of his own mansion in the back of a van unseen by anyone?

Maybe there was plenty of people who wished him a great ill, and yet, the conversation was so benign. As Catriona tucked into her chicken, she heard the woman discuss the intricacies of finding a snowsuit that fitted. Her skis were fading after a number of years as they didn't cut through the ice the way they used to. Having skied herself, Cat was well aware of what skis could do, how they can make a fool of you, but inside her mind was churning.

Where were the jewels? The woman had left her handbag down by her feet and was seemingly paying no attention to it. Maybe she had them in a pocket in the skirt. Cat had no idea. If only Tiff was here to talk it over with. Where did people keep these things? She didn't have them around her neck. Cat was wondering where exactly she could have hidden them. Did the skirt have pockets? It didn't seem so. It must be in the handbag, surely, or did she leave them out in the car?

Cat's eyes cast over to the man sitting four tables away. It was the same man who had accompanied his boss the day before. Cat wondered what weapons he had on his person. Would he be able to shoot here? Would he be bothered about drawing a weapon whilst being in public? Was the man that well-feared? Clearly, the staff were nervous serving him, but that was understandable—some of them could lose their jobs. Surely, that would be a problem, never mind losing their lives, but maybe he tipped well. Cat found her mind was wandering, wandering away because she was trying not to make a decision. What should she do? Grab the bag, or sit here and watch him play out?

Cat got to her feet and made her way towards the restroom inside the restaurant. The jewels were in the bag. They had to be. She had to take the handbag and go. Once inside one of the ladies' cubicles, Cat shed her outer clothing and emerged wearing black trousers and a black top. The hat was gone. She now let her hair hang down before tying it up in a ponytail at the back. It needed to look functional. In a rear pocket of her trousers was a notebook and a pen, a little detail that Tiff had noted. 'If you wanted to look the part, you had to really look the part.'

Catriona bent down and washed her hands in the cold water from the tap of the washbasin in the women's washroom. She heard the door open and kept her head down as the blonde-haired woman walked in, making her way to one of the toilet cubicles. Cat fought to stop herself from shaking, but she also knew this was a good time, one less person with eyes on her. Steeling herself, she exited the washroom, made her way through the restaurant, and out to the open-air area, walking directly to the table of the man in the silver suit.

'Can I get you anything else, sir?' she asked in Italian and saw the man look up and beam at her.

'New here?' he asked, and Catriona nodded. 'Excellent,' he said. 'Maybe you can do the run-up to the house next time we take out.' Catriona saw a sneer on him and was aware the man was casting his eyes up and down her full figure. He reached forward, dropping his napkin on the floor. 'Can you can get that for me, please?' he asked.

Catriona was well aware of the oldest trick in the book, but she also thought that this was a time to initiate her plan. Bending over, she felt a hand on her rear. As gross as it was, she ignored it, reaching down instead, and grabbing the handbag by the chair opposite the man. Standing upright, she turned, keeping the bag behind her with one hand and handing the man back his napkin with the other.

'You seem very suitable,' he said. 'I take it you're a tourist working to earn your keep?'

Catriona smiled, 'Yes, sir, travelling through the train with my brother during our tour of Europe over the next couple of years.'

'Excellent,' said the man. 'We shall see more of you.'

'I look forward to it, sir,' said Catriona, and calmly turned back moving the bag to her front. She felt a pinch on her bottom and walked off, aware that her shoulders had tensed. She needed to stay calm, keep with the plan. She looked to her left and saw Tiff on the far side of the bank. Walking over to the wall that enclosed the outdoor area, Cat huddled around the bag, opening the clasp on it, and looking inside.

There was a hairbrush, something that resonated with Cat, as well as a number of nail files and other beauty products, but there was also a small bag sitting in the middle. Cat reached down gently and prised it open. The gleam of the jewels inside was obvious. She tied the bag back up, taking the small bag in her hand while closing the clasp on the handbag.

'Who the hell are you?' came a booming voice from across the tables. Cat looked over her shoulder and saw who she presumed to be the restaurant manager. The man in the silver suit stood up and Cat saw the man wave to his bodyguard who came running over towards him.

She would have to move. She put her hand on the wall, swung her legs up onto it and, grabbing the bag, rolled off the other side. Cat landed on her feet and, thankfully, wasn't wearing the high-heeled shoes most of the rest of the staff were.

Instead, she had a pair of smart black boots on, and she began to run along the riverside.

There was a cry of, 'Get her,' from behind in Italian. Cat took the handbag and flung it as hard as she could across the small river. It landed on the bank on the far side, and she saw Tiff making her way towards it. Cat didn't stop to see what would happen, instead, running further along the riverbank before cutting inside, up the back alley of a house and out into the streets of the village.

It wasn't the largest village in the area, but it did have a small maze of older buildings. Back in the days, the lower-class people were all shoved together in small houses, peasants working the fields while the largest mansion houses took in all the reward. She had a brief thought of Luigi's family and almost felt guilty about it, but there was no time to think about the past; the present was in front of her, and she could hear the shouts of people following.

The man in the silver suit would no doubt have plenty of people. He could come out and begin a hunt. She also thought about this. While she may not have trusted the police entirely, she made sure that Tiff had placed a call to them as soon as she saw the blonde woman coming in for lunch, and it clearly worked because she saw a police car now and found herself having to cut up a different alley to stay away from it.

The police were not there to give the jewels to, the police were there to deter anyone from firing guns at her, for the pursuit to be less rigid. Cat was turning back in a loop, believing that rather than run away from everyone, if she cut back towards them, she would confuse them. She made her way down a small alley with high overhanging buildings and came out at a town square. It was small and only called so because the local council offices were at one end. In the middle was a large well, entitled 'The Water of Life' by a placard by the side.

It was a place for tourists even though it wasn't well known, a place like every village had, somewhere to make a buck out of people. At this one, people would throw money, coins, and make a wish. Cat wished she could just jump into it and turn up somewhere else, but as she went across the square, she saw the blonde-haired woman on the far side. She was holding a gun and had two goons beside her.

'He said to me that you were dead. He won't make that mistake again. All he had to do was kill you at the roadside, and yet, here you are, interrupting my dinner.' Cat realised that the woman was not Italian, for the way she spoke the language was stilted. Not so much that it couldn't be understood, but she didn't have the easy-flowing style of Luigi or his family, or indeed, that of the man she had been to dinner with.

'The police are in the village. I'll just walk out and give them this,' said Cat, holding up the small bag she had taken from the handbag.

'I don't think you will,' said the woman. 'If you look behind you, I think you'll see someone you know.'

Catriona turned around and was shocked to see Tiff standing there, a man beside her, holding a gun to her side. Cat moved towards the well, trying to put something between herself and the blonde-haired woman. She watched the woman attaching a silencer to her gun.

'You see, it ends here. Many things disappeared in that well. Many wishes are cast. It's deep. They won't find you down there. A quick shot to the head would throw you over, you and your sister.' High in such a moment, the feeling of pride of being seen as a sister and not an aunt, caused Cat to smile much to the bafflement of her attackers, and to her own surprise. Maybe it was that time in life when you just went for it; you just had to play the part.

Turning around, Cat saw Tiff being brought forward, and she knew she had to seize the moment somehow. Would the police rush in? Who knew? Cat took the jewels, placed the bag on the edge of the well before placing her hand inside it.

'Stop. If it's that deep, you won't find these either. You move closer, I drop them.' With that, she put one hand in the bag, lifted out the jewels, and held them in her closed hand over the top of the well. The small bag that had contained them, she stuffed into her trousers.

'It's your call. Let my sister come to me or I drop these.'

'And do what when you drop them?' sneered the blonde-haired woman. 'It's just us; we'll still kill you.'

'You won't if you want these. I'll leave them here on the well and we'll walk away.'

'But you won't, will you?' said the woman. 'You'll keep coming back. You've got a stake in this somehow. I don't know why but you've tracked across Europe to achieve your goal.'

'I was attached to these jewels, but now I know the story, it doesn't matter. You won't have them. I won't have them.'

'Ah, but you won't do it now, will you?' queried the blonde-haired woman. 'You prize it too much.'

'My sister to me now,' said Cat, 'or I'll let go.'

The woman shook her head. Cat opened her hand quickly and the jewels began to drop, but she snapped it closed again before they could fall from her hand.

'Next time it stays open. Bring her here.' The woman nodded

at the goon behind Cat. Turning around, Cat saw Tiff being ushered to her. She was shaking, but Cat didn't move her hand from the well, keeping the jewels hanging over it.

'Now, we have a stalemate,' said the woman. 'Nowhere to go. Drop them, I win, you die. Walk away, I come for you, you die. You have to stay there the whole time just holding them over that well. At some point you'll lose, at some point.'

'Help, help,' cried Tiff, 'She's collapsed. She's collapsed.'

Her sudden cry was taking everyone by surprise, and the woman didn't know what to do.

'Police, help. Police, ambulance, somebody, help,' cried Tiff in English.

Cat saw policemen start to emerge from the far passageway and instantly let go of the jewels, dropping them into the well. She let herself fall to the floor, lying there, as if she'd collapsed. With her eyes closed, she couldn't see what was happening. She felt Tiff's hand upon her head, and then there was a whisper of, 'Don't get up. Just lie there. I've got this. Start to open your eyes in a minute.'

Cat heard somebody rushing up beside Tiff. He first of all asked in Italian was she all right, and then a hand came down, touching her. Cat opened her eyes and saw the police officer. There was another one behind him. As Cat was helped to her feet, she looked around, but suddenly, there were no goons—there was no blonde-haired woman.

Tiff insisted that the police officers help them, take them out to the nearest hospital where Catriona was given a check-up. They were nervous, wondering if anyone would follow, but no one did.

As soon as Cat was discharged from the hospital, the pair boarded a train and made their way straight to the airport.

Catriona booked a flight departing in two hours for London and then made a phone call. She spoke in Italian, describing herself as a blonde-haired woman, someone with remorse for what she had done. She told of the jewels she had dropped in the well. Cat didn't say much more. She didn't need to. Instead, she sat in the departure lounge at a small bar made out to be something classier than it was, and took the first cocktail off the list.

'We did it. We got away,' said Tiff.

'We did,' said Cat, 'but we lost the jewels. We're not going to be able to clear Luigi's name.'

'We might yet,' said Tiff. 'We might yet.'

23

Chapter 23

Catriona removed the blonde wig and placed it on the table beside a red one her niece had taken off moments before. She carefully undid the suit she was wearing, hanging it up in the ornate wardrobe in the far corner of the twin bedroom. The style of the room was grandiose and a little too backward for her taste, but she had no doubt that the man who had given them the room had done it out of the goodness of his heart. Finally, they had made it back to Scotland and were keeping their heads down, back at the family home for a week.

In the weeks that followed, Cat had received a call from Alberto. It appeared that they had tried to dig up the well. Certain criminal elements have been found trying to get to the bottom of the well and dredge it out, but given the size of it, their operations were difficult and attracted a lot of attention. A phone call, made by an anonymous Italian, which had directed the police towards this well had also helped in placing pressure on those who were trying to dig it out. Thus, certain criminal elements were picked up and arrested.

When the authorities took over the operation and found four jewels, four of the five that had been stolen from a Milan bank many years ago, they started to piece a story together. Of course, the press in Italy gave much more than the basic facts and the police could never guarantee exactly who had been involved, but certain references were made to the son of a certain high-ranking official in the local area.

The sad part of the story was that the cobra's fang, one of the items of jewellery, was still missing. Despite having excavated, the fang had apparently disappeared through the watercourse that ran underneath the village. It could be almost anywhere, and no one was going to dig up an entire town to find one jewel. The other four were reunited with the bank in Milan and Alberto had then called Catriona, asking her to come over to see it. Cat wasn't sure if he was simply trying to see if his old friend's wife was up for a new life, but he had been gracious none the same.

Tiff had joined Cat, and while they travelled under some dubious Italian passports, they were nonetheless both entertained by Alberto in style. Catriona visited the small village she had found him in, and over several nights, he had talked with her about the old times. Tiff had been bored, but she was glad to be in the area. Under a false-red bonnet, Tiff had also gone to see the house she had wanted to break into. When Cat found out that she was looking at the crime boss's mansion, studying it, trying to see his reaction, she nearly flipped the lid, but instead, she brought her niece back and made her read the reports in the Italian press of a certain blonde woman who had been found trying to swim too long underwater. If Cat ever needed a reminder of how deadly the company she was mixing in was, that was it.

Because of that, Tiff stayed closer to Alberto. Over a couple of weeks, he took them around various sites where Luigi had grown up, some places Cat had never visited. But they kept coming back to the village where Cat had dropped the jewels.

'Do you want to look for it?' Alberto had asked in the village. 'If you want to, we'll dig up, we'll excavate, we'll look for it.'

'That would be awfully strange,' said Cat. 'Why would you be doing that? Why suddenly swan in here and help? I know you have money, but it would look strange. I wouldn't want to involve you any further than I have.'

'But you must miss him, and you must miss it. You can't have that much of Luigi left. Not the close things.'

Cat nodded as she'd walked over to the renovated well and looked down before turning around, placing a hand on Alberto's cheek.

'You dear, dear man,' she said. 'But you can't understand that once you've lost the person, nothing else matters. Everything else is shallow.' Tiff had then interrupted them with numerous drawings of watercourses and where she thought that the cobra's fang would end up. Suddenly, she was a water engineer. Cat, although she was convinced that Tiff probably didn't have it fully right, knew that her niece would have more of a clue than she did.

The day of the great trip to Milan came where there was a large presentation in the hall of the bank, one Alberto had been invited to, or at least had managed to get his name on with a plus two. Of course, the last thing that Cat wanted to do was to appear in public like this, aware that the authorities had seen someone like her collapse near the well. A random chance, a glimpse of someone like her, two and two put together, and suddenly, the heat would be back on and she'd have a lot of explaining to do. So far, the chaos they had caused throughout Europe hadn't come back to them. But as it happened, the day passed off peacefully and Cat felt glad that the bank was again the rightful custodian of the now smaller family of jewels.

Catriona turned to her wardrobe and took out a summer dress with a light blouse and looked in the mirror as she made herself up. Tiff had already slapped on a pair of jeans and a large jumper that seemed to be quite hot for the heat in Italy, but Cat was taking her time. A knock at the door broke her moment's reflection in the mirror. On opening it, she saw Alberto standing outside, wearing a crisp blue shirt and some pale trousers.

'So where do we go next?' asked Alberto. 'Where can I take you in this country of mine?'

'I'll see you out on the balcony in a moment,' said Cat. 'I think our time here may have run out.'

'No, no, no,' said Alberto. 'We'll discuss it outside. Come, the sun is shining. It deserves to have its glory bathe on a woman like you.'

'Your flattery will get you nowhere,' said Cat, 'but please, continue. Just give me a moment to powder my nose.'

And with that, she dismissed him, aware that she'd kept him on a leash over these last few weeks. The man had been so helpful, but his underlying intention was clear to her.

She found him honourable, decent, but she had no real love for Alberto. A good neighbour. A friend, certainly, but nothing more.

Over the previous months, after Luigi's death, Cat had found her heart occasionally pulled this way and that, but she realised that all these things were just the reaction of a lonely person.

She needed to be at peace with Luigi's passing. She needed to have time. When would the men realise that the last thing she wanted was another man? Still, as a woman with money, and hopefully the looks, Catriona was bound to entertain suitors, bound to have men coming and asking, but at least Alberto had been civilised about it.

She made her way out to the balcony, where a glass of something with bubbles in it was handed to her. Alberto toasted to her health.

'So where should we go?' he said. 'Where in this great land of mine can I take you?'

'You can take me tomorrow to the airport and we'll fly back to Scotland.' Cat watched the disappointment in the man's face. 'I know what you're thinking, and I want to say thank you, Alberto. You've done so much for us. You've given us a chance to be here, to see everything close up. I do truly feel now that after all our exploits, we are clear. Your crime boss has not made a move at all. He's not even looking for us. He just dispatched that poor woman.'

'Poor woman?' said Alberto. 'She put a gun to your head. She ordered someone else to kill you. She's not that poor.'

'She is now. And you've been so good with Tiff. A lot of people struggle to entertain her. She's quite rude and abrupt at times, but it's never bothered you.'

'She is certainly interesting,' said Alberto, 'but you wouldn't be here without her. Entertaining her is a price I'm delighted to pay. But tell me, Contessa, Catriona, you must be lonely.'

Catriona took a large swig out of her wine glass and placed it on the edge of the balcony. 'Of course, I'm lonely. I'm very lonely. That's not a hole you can fill, Alberto. It's not a hole anyone can fill at the moment. It's a hole I need to go and examine, tear apart to live. Then maybe one day, I'll look again. Maybe one day, I'll be ready, but until then, my companion is over there, because she reminds me that there's more than me to look after in this life.'

'Dare I say, I'll be waiting.'

'You can dare, but I wouldn't, Alberto. Who knows, I may end up happy with this. Being a widow might suit me.' The man's face was shocked until he saw Cat's smile. 'Thank you,' she said and reached up to kiss the man on the cheek.

'Now, what do we do for the rest of the day?' he asked.

'Let's just enjoy the sunshine,' said Cat. 'Let's rest on our labours. The bank has four of the jewels. They're happy, the police are happy. The full story of the robbery is known, dug out by the press. The involvement of Luigi's fellow dueller, is now known. My husband's name is clear. It's time to rest, Alberto, time to just enjoy the sunshine now that it's finally come.'

'Then, to you and to your niece,' said Alberto, 'and I hope that one day I'll see you here again.'

Cat grabbed her glass, reached up with it and touched it to Alberto's, so that the glassware rang in the sunshine. Cat took another sip of her wine, smiled at Alberto, and then turned away to look out into the countryside. She wasn't ready to rest yet. There was one more thing to do. 'Oh, Alberto,' said Cat, turning around again. 'I do you have one favour to ask.'

'Name it,' said Alberto. 'You just have to ask.'

'My niece likes a halfpipe. I don't know if you know them. It's for snowboards, competitions and that. I just don't feel up to it at the moment. I want you to take her on a week's skiing.'

'Of course,' said Alberto. 'I can do that, but why don't you come and join us?'

'I'd love to,' said Tiff. 'But I can't. I've got somebody I need to go and see, a goodbye to say.'

'Are they dying?' asked Alberto. 'You have that look on your face like they're dying.'

'I certainly won't be seeing much of them in the time to come,' said Cat. 'That much is true.'

24

Epilogue

Catriona stepped out of the tin bath. It had been a long time since she had to boil water and place it inside a bath. Nowadays everything was Jacuzzis or power showers but there was a time when she'd come up here, away from it all. There had been the hassle of her family, the hassle of his family, and here for a week, they had found themselves. It was just before they decided to get married, a time to talk, a time to work out what to do when so much was against them.

Taking a towel, Cat rubbed herself down, drying off as best she could. There were a number of logs crackling in the stove and the log cabin was certainly warm, but there was no power, only fire to heat things, to keep herself warm. There was no mobile phone signal, nothing at all. In fact, the nearest cabin was a good two to three miles away.

Catriona wrapped herself up in the white dressing gown, fluffy and furry and snug as anything. She looked at the matching one in the wardrobe that would no longer be put on. She remembered stepping out of the bath before drying herself, going to reach for a dressing gown and being told by Luigi that one was enough for the pair of them. They had come to one mind up here, come to one body, come to be one, and until that awful day when he was taken from her, the pair were inseparable.

Catriona felt a tear running down her cheek as she sniffed hard. She looked at the small balcony right outside the log cabin windows and made her way slowly out there. The snow was lying all around, and the air was crisp and cold, but wrapped up in the dressing gown, she felt brave enough to face it. Part of her was shivering inside because this was the part she didn't want to do. Taking a bottle of tequila from the floor of the balcony, Cat plonked herself down on a wooden rocking chair.

She remembered it well. They'd sat in it together. His lap was always comfortable, but now she sat in it alone, staring off at a sun that was fleeting, starting to descend behind a mountain. She took the top off of the tequila bottle and didn't bother with a cup, drinking down large gulps before putting it back on the floor beside her. Unsteadily she stood up, walked to the edge of the balcony.

'I know you're gone, but I know you see me. I miss you. My love, I miss you.' Bowing her head, Cat began to cry, doubling over all of a sudden like she'd been punched in the stomach. Her body wracked with the memory of something so good that she shuddered, eventually dropping to her knees as the tears flowed. It was two minutes later when she picked herself up, her dressing gown dishevelled. She stood in the cool air, drawing the gown back so the nape of her neck and further down was exposed. Her hand disappeared inside the dressing gown pocket and pulled out a small bag. It had previously been in the handbag of the blonde lady who now swam with the fishes, as the TV dramas like to say.

Cat delicately opened the bag and took out a necklace before letting the bag drop off of the balcony out into the snow. The necklace had a chain which she attached around her neck so that it hung right down the nape, and with her other hand, she checked the pendant that was hanging from it. It was in the shape of a snake with an emerald behind it.

'You fought for me, my love,' she shouted, 'for me,' and she held the cobra's fang up to the dying sun. She poured out her defiance. The tears came back, and Catriona knew there would be more grieving to come.

Read on to discover the Patrick Smythe series!

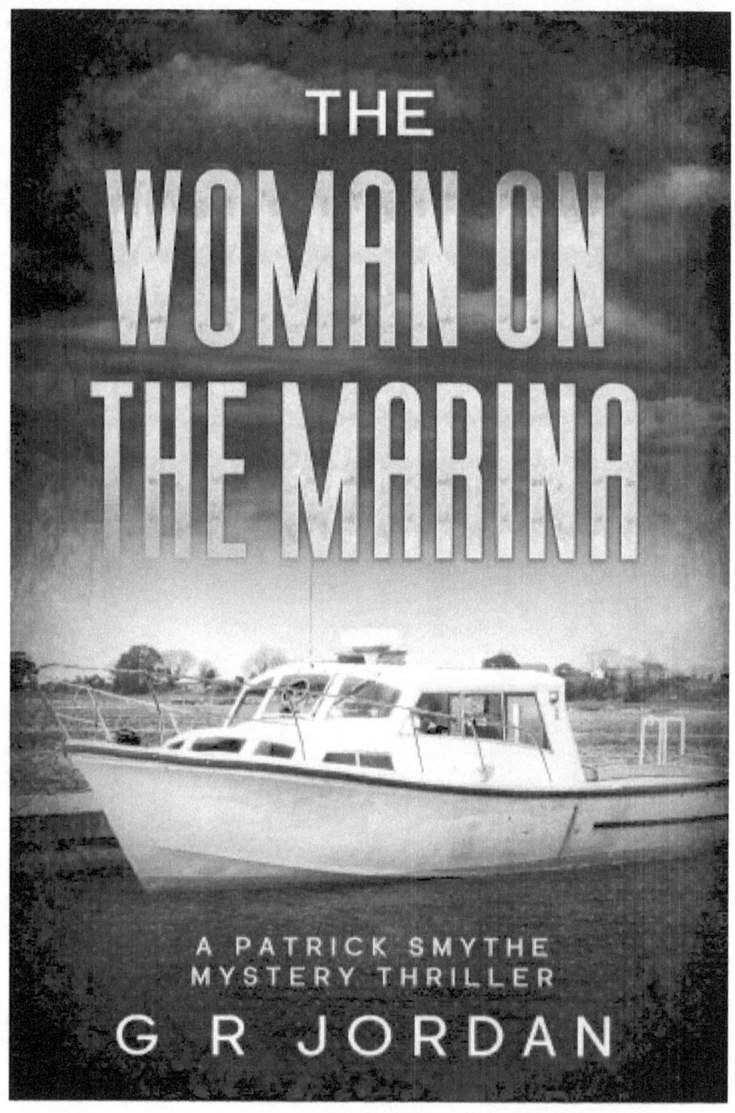

Start your Patrick Smythe journey here!

Patrick Smythe is a former Northern Irish policeman who

after suffering an amputation after a bomb blast, takes to the sea between the west coast of Scotland and his homeland to ply his trade as a private investigator. Join Paddy as he tries to work to his own ethics while knowing how to bend the rules he once enforced. Working from his beloved motorboat 'Craigantlet', Paddy decides to rescue a drug mule in this short story from the pen of G R Jordan.

Join G R Jordan's monthly newsletter about forthcoming releases and special writings for his tribe of avid readers and then receive your free Patrick Smythe short story.

Go to https://bit.ly/PatrickSmythe for your Patrick Smythe journey to start!

About the Author

GR Jordan is a self-published author who finally decided at forty that in order to have an enjoyable lifestyle, his creative beast within would have to be unleashed. His books mirror that conflict in life where acts of decency contend with self-promotion, goodness stares in horror at evil, and kindness blindsides us when we at our worst. Corrupting our world with his parade of wondrous and horrific characters, he highlights everyday tensions with fresh eyes whilst taking his methodical, intelligent mainstays on a roller-coaster ride of dilemmas, all the while suffering the banter of their provocative sidekicks.

A graduate of Loughborough University where he masqueraded as a chemical engineer but ultimately played American football, Gary had worked at changing the shape of cereal flakes and pulled a pallet truck for a living. Watching vegetables freeze at -40'C was another career highlight and he was also one of the Scottish Highlands "blind" air traffic controllers.

These days he has graduated to answering a telephone to people in trouble before telephoning other people to sort it out.

Having flirted with most places in the UK, he is now based in the Isle of Lewis in Scotland where his free time is spent between raising a young family with his wife, writing, figuring out how to work a loom and caring for a small flock of chickens. Luckily, his writing is influenced by his varied work and life experience as the chickens have not been the poetical inspiration he had hoped for!

You can connect with me on:

○ https://grjordan.com

f https://facebook.com/carpetlessleprechaun

Subscribe to my newsletter:

✉ https://bit.ly/PatrickSmythe

Also by G R Jordan

G R Jordan writes across multiple genres including crime, dark and action adventure fantasy, feel good fantasy, mystery thriller and horror fantasy. Below is a selection of his work. Whilst all books are available across online stores, signed copies are available at his personal shop.

A Shot at Democracy: A Kirsten Stewart Thriller #1

https://grjordan.com/product/a-shot-at-democracy

A whisper on the wind tells of murderous intent. An assassin prepares in the highlands. Can new operative Kirsten Stewart hunt down the killer before they strike at the heart of Scotland's democracy.

Having left the Highlands murder team behind and joined the shadowy world of the secret services, former DC Kirsten Stewart overhears a plot that strikes to the very core of Scotland's governance. As the stakes get higher and Kirsten becomes cut off from her superiors, can she stop the assassin before they eliminate their prime target.

In her first solo mission, Kirsten Stewart finds herself in deep shadow and in receipt of disturbing news. Only by remaining incommunicado can she find out the intentions of a killer and stop the murder of Scotland's top politician. Will former boss DI Macleod's faith in her be justified or will she watch the deadliest attack on Scotland's democracy happen on her watch?

To work without a net, you must face the fear of falling!

Highlands and Islands Detective Thriller Series

https://grjordan.com/product/waters-edge

Join stalwart DI Macleod and his burgeoning new DC McGrath as they look into the darker side of the stunningly scenic and wilder parts of the north of Scotland. From the Black Isle to Lewis, from Mull to Harris and across to the small Isles, the Uists and Barra, this mismatched pairing follow murders, thieves and vengeful victims in an effort to restore tranquillity to the remoter parts of the land.

Be part of this tale of a surprise partnership amidst the foulest deeds and darkest souls who stalk this peaceful and most beautiful of lands, and you'll never see the Highlands the same way again.

The Patrick Smythe Trilogy – Irish private Investigator on Scotland's West Coast

Patrick Smythe is a former Northern Irish policeman who despite suffering an amputation after a bomb blast, takes to the sea between the west coast of Scotland and his homeland to ply his trade as a private investigator. Join Paddy as he tries to work to his own ethics while knowing how to bend the rules he once enforced. Working from his beloved motorboat 'Craigantlet', Paddy takes on a string of cases, finds a new colleague and even manages to rekindle his love-life while bringing the guilty to justice.

If you love pacey action, suspicious motives, and devious characters, then Paddy Smythe operates amongst your kind of people.

Austerley & Kirkgordon Adventures Box Set

https://grjordan.com/product/ak-box-set

A retired bodyguard looking for a little fun before it's too late. An obsessive Professor, seeking the darkest things of life. And an Elder god arriving to rule the world, if they can't stop him.

Join Austerley and Kirkgordon on the rollercoaster ride that is their first three adventures. Comprising 3 full novels as well as three accompanying origin novellettes, this collection will introduce you to a polarised duo that are the world's best hope. Joining them for the adventure are a myriad of strange characters, bizarre anmals, evil humans and the UK's finest agents from its most secret department.

As one reviewer put it, "If you like Lovecraft, Poe, or Conan Doyle you will like this book. If you like tv show like Buffy the Vampire Slayer, Supernatural, Being Human, or X-Files you will like this book."

So take a chance on a molotov cocktail of a duo and see how to save the world on the wild side.

www.ingramcontent.com/pod-product-compliance
Lightning Source LLC
Chambersburg PA
CBHW030753190726
48285CB00003B/838